S0-BOI-055

Murder in Containment

PENNY LEINWANDER

iUniverse, Inc.
New York   Bloomington

Murder in Containment

Copyright © 2009 Penny Leinwander

All rights reserved. No part of this book may be used or reproduced by any means, graphic, electronic, or mechanical, including photocopying, recording, taping or by any information storage retrieval system without the written permission of the publisher except in the case of brief quotations embodied in critical articles and reviews.

This is a work of fiction. All of the characters, names, incidents, organizations, and dialogue in this novel are either the products of the author's imagination or are used fictitiously.

iUniverse books may be ordered through booksellers or by contacting:

iUniverse
1663 Liberty Drive
Bloomington, IN 47403
www.iuniverse.com
1-800-Authors (1-800-288-4677)

Because of the dynamic nature of the Internet, any Web addresses or links contained in this book may have changed since publication and may no longer be valid. The views expressed in this work are solely those of the author and do not necessarily reflect the views of the publisher, and the publisher hereby disclaims any responsibility for them.

ISBN: 978-1-4401-7273-1 (pbk)
ISBN: 978-1-4401-7271-7 (cloth)
ISBN: 978-1-4401-7272-4 (ebk)

Printed in the United States of America

iUniverse rev. date: 10/14/2009

To Mark and Danielle

Chapter 1

CHRIS SIEVERS CLOSED THE PERSONNEL hatch and turned the oversized wheel until a small green light nearby illuminated. Lindy Andrews, who was standing next to Chris, felt the pressure change on her eardrums once the airtight seal was achieved.

Chris and Lindy were inside a small tubular compartment with large round hatches at each end, one opening to the auxiliary building that they had just left, and the other opening to the containment building of the West Isles Nuclear Power Plant. The indicator light bathed the airlock compartment in green, overpowering the dim white light that came from the lightbulb hanging from the ceiling. The quiet roar of mechanical equipment beyond the containment hatch could be felt more than heard.

One step closer to getting out of here," Lindy thought to herself as she turned to see Chris cranking open the opposite hatch wheel that led to the containment building. The open steel grating that served as the floor of the compartment snagged her rubber boots when she turned to face Chris. She felt herself getting woozy; the feeling of claustrophobia began to build in the pit of her stomach. Locked, confined spaces made her feel uneasy, out of control. Lindy steadied herself by concentrating on the actions she would take once the containment hatch was opened. She wanted to get this job done as quickly as possible so she wouldn't have to be with Chris any longer than necessary. It was an uncomfortable situation, and she wished she hadn't been the one assigned to provide the radiation safety escort for this containment entry. Chris had moved out of her house just two weeks ago, after they decided to end their relationship and go their separate ways. She missed Chris and was now finding it hard to work with him, knowing that this was as close as they would get from now on. She didn't want to look at him or at his gorgeous blue eyes. She missed his strong voice and his goofy grin. She missed his killer lasagna on Saturday nights and the way he yelled at the television when he disagreed with a news analyst. She sighed. Right now, she couldn't remember what they had fought about or why he had moved out. Whose fault was it? Hers? His? He was the one with the short fuse. True, she spoke her mind, but he was the one who always left his dirty socks on the floor and never called to say he'd be late.

When Lindy heard that she was assigned to the job of escorting Chris into the containment building, she considered stomping into Al Jensen's office and complaining about unfair treatment. Obviously, someone in the radiation protection office had thought it would be funny to have her working together with Chris after their breakup. Providing a safety escort for a power entry was not part of her normal job, after all; she was a radiological engineer and worked on projects. Jobs that involved radioactive systems had to be covered by a radiation protection technician, hence the term escort. She didn't do grunt work like escorting workers into containment. But after some thought, Lindy realized that storming into Jensen's office was exactly what the radiation protection technicians wanted her to do. Getting her goat was their goal. Knowing this, she decided to play it as if she didn't mind. Jerry and Thumper had been loitering near Jensen's office, probably hoping to catch her tantrum. She had enjoyed their look of disappointment when she casually walked by Jensen's office without stopping and headed to the dressing room to get ready for the entry.

Making containment entries while the nuclear plant was producing power was not routine at the West Isles plant, and because of the hazardous environment inside containment, such entries required full respiratory and safety gear, including a hazmat suit made out of Tyvek. Tyvek is sturdy but thin material, lightweight and impervious to moisture. In the dim light, Lindy could hardly see Chris's face through the plastic face cover of his respirator. No verbal communication was possible. Chris turned toward Lindy. Was he trying to say something? She hoped so, but talk was impossible at this point. He reached toward her but then turned back toward the wheel and continued cranking. Earlier Lindy and Chris had spent an hour sealing themselves in sturdy outerwear to prevent contact with the containment environment they were soon to enter. Just before donning her respirator and entering the containment hatch, Lindy had carefully glanced at Chris, hoping that he was watching her and she could make an excuse to talk with him, but he wasn't. Let him make the first move, she thought. He was the one who'd moved out.

Chris made one more turn on the wheel. There was a slight popping sensation on her eardrums as the inner hatch opened. The sound of electrical equipment instantly filled the entry compartment; it was deafening but energizing at the same time. The sudden increase in moisture and temperature was immediately apparent, even through the protective Tyvek suits. After checking her radiation meter, Lindy stepped over the hatch lip onto the honeycombed steel grating of the containment building.

The south containment hatch airlock was one of two entry points into the containment building at the West Isles plant. The containment building housed the reactor vessel and the equipment used to generate the steam that drives the turbines to make electricity. The containment building was designed to keep radioactive material from escaping to the outside world in the event of an accident. Although the two containment hatches allowed entry, there was no direct opening to the outside. The West Isles containment structure was round with a domed top, rising some twenty stories above ground level. The walls were eight solid feet of high-density concrete reinforced with rebar the size of tree limbs. The design specifications for the dome required that even in the worst-case scenario, such as a direct hit by a 747, the dome would not rupture and a leak would not occur. Lindy had no doubt that this specification had been met.

Containment entries reminded Lindy of what it would be like to be under the hood of an automobile with the engine running. A foggy gray mist hung in the open spaces, making the nuclear steam supply components appear hazy and distant, even though they were only a few yards away. Lindy felt energized in the building. She wondered whether it was because the electrical power running the pumps and other equipment was enough to power a small city by themselves. Or perhaps it was because West Isles generated enough power to meet the needs of the entire population in the southern half of the state.

Lindy squinted. Through the haze she saw the walkway located near the curved inside wall of containment. Lindy was required to lead the way in these first moments since she carried the most important piece of safety equipment, the radiation meter. Remote monitors indicated acceptable levels in containment, but she needed to verify it. Chris carefully followed her past the dense network of piping and equipment to a stairwell that led down to the minus-10 level of the building, ten feet below ground level. At the bottom of the stairs there was more piping and equipment, which they gingerly walked around so as to avoid contact with their suits. Contamination on their suits would complicate their exit at the step-off pad later. As they walked, Lindy thought about the last two weeks without Chris. She had cleaned out closets and painted her bedroom, but still she couldn't shake her loneliness. She didn't want Chris to know that, though.

Several minutes later they reached their destination: the northeast sump. Chris, a reactor operator, had been sent to inspect this sump because there had been a small but measurable amount of liquid accumulating in it over the last several days. The floor on this level was concrete. The sump was a five-foot square pit in the concrete floor. The floors were sloped so that any stray liquid would collect in the pit, and the sensor in the bottom of the pit reported to the control room the level of any liquid present. The source of this liquid had baffled the plant engineers. For the past five years of plant operations, this sump had remained dry. None of the plant systems that used water indicated any loss of volume, and leak rates of gallons per minute were of more concern than the small quantity that had been detected here in the northeast sump. The leak rate clearly did not exceed operating limits, but a closer look was needed to ensure it wasn't an indication of something worse to come.

While Lindy kept an eye on the radiation levels, which were reading higher, as expected for the area, Chris used his flashlight to look for the source of the liquid. Liquid was trickling into the sump from a source on the far left side, behind an electrical panel. Chris tapped Lindy on the shoulder and pointed to the trail of liquid. Lindy nodded and followed Chris as he proceeded to take a closer look. Lindy kept one eye on Chris and one eye on the meter. Since the reactor vessel was located just beyond the concrete shield a couple of feet ahead of them, there could be a radiation hot spot in the vicinity. Suddenly Chris stopped, causing Lindy to bump into him. Lindy looked over his shoulder and saw what looked like a white Tyvek protective suit tucked behind the electrical equipment. It appeared to be the source of the liquid.

Lindy wished she could speak to Chris and ask him why a Tyvek suit would be stuffed in a corner, but all she could do was watch as Chris crouched down and pulled on the material. He dislodged a large lump. Lindy, caught by surprise, stepped back and turned away, pulling off her respirator and face mask before she vomited. With the mask off, the smell of rotting flesh was overwhelming and made her more nauseated. Why hadn't she kept her mask on when she saw the decomposing human head protruding from the collar of the suit?

Chapter 2

MARCUS LAIDEN WAS THE SHIFT supervisor on duty at the West Isles plant. He sat in his office with a big binder on his lap and the handset of the phone cradled on his shoulder. Outside his office was the control room where two reactor operators were scanning electrical panels that covered the four walls from floor to ceiling. The operators occasionally turned a knob or flipped a switch.

"I can't find a tech spec that covers this," Marcus said while turning pages in the binder. "Discovering a body just isn't addressed by any tech spec that I can find." He reached for the cigarette resting in the ashtray on his desk and took a long drag; an inch-long ash hung precariously before dropping onto the floor.

Marcus was on the phone with Ira Showalter, the resident inspector. Ira was a nuclear engineer assigned by the United States Nuclear Regulatory Commission to "assist West Isles with the safe operation of the plant." A resident inspector was located at every nuclear plant in the country; their proximity allowed them to report violations to NRC headquarters in Washington DC immediately. The NRC was not shy about issuing violations and fines for misconduct by the facilities.

Ira was at his home looking through his own copy of the West Isles technical specification manual. Although the manual contained over five hundred pages, he was intimately familiar with the technical requirements on those pages, as was the shift supervisor. Each page specified an operating condition, such as the maximum operating temperature allowed for the reactor core. Many technical specifications limits were mundane and addressed such requirements as the number of backup power sources available during operation. Each requirement had to be met for the power plant to stay at power and online. Everything imaginable was addressed in the binder that Marcus had on his lap, including even the weather conditions that the power plant was allowed to operate under.

"Why me?" Ira asked himself. He had worked for eight years as an inspector for the commission, and he had never heard of an incident involving a dead body, let alone a dead body found in containment after the plant had returned to power. This was certainly going to cost him sleep, and it was such bad timing. He was in the process of having a new home built.

"Who's the dead guy?" he asked irritably, "and how could you possibly have left someone in containment and not know it?"

"Look, I don't know how this happened or who the person is, but it certainly looks like it was done on purpose, because the body wasn't supposed to be found. And it wouldn't have been if the body fluids hadn't collected in a sump that's normally bone dry," said Marcus.

"Real funny," replied the inspector, sarcastically.

"Hey, I've got fifteen minutes to make a decision. Do you have anything to help me out here?" asked Marcus, feeling the pressure of the time limit and not noticing that the filterless cigarette was about to burn his fingers. One of the pages in the technical manual specified that any unusual events had to be called into the NRC operations center within fifteen minutes.

"Well, it may not be spelled out in any specific tech spec, but this incident has to qualify as an emergency, but what level, I'm not sure," said Ira.

Marcus finally noticed the cigarette burning his fingers and threw the butt into the ashtray. Except for this slip, Marcus remained calm, despite facing this tough situation and the time constraint. His time in the navy as an operator for a nuclear submarine had made running a nuclear power plant above sea level a piece of cake. At least mistakes above water didn't end up with your crewmates dead. As shift supervisor, he had complete authority over the plant, but he was also ultimately responsible for all actions taken. Shutting the plant down would cost the utility millions in lost revenue, but not making the right decision could cost a million in fines from the NRC. There was also the more costly risk of losing the confidence of the public. Everything that happened at the plant made it into the local papers.

"Okay," said Marcus, "I'm going to classify this as a security breach. Someone's in the containment building who shouldn't be there, even though he's not in any condition to do any harm."

"Hey! Good idea. I hadn't thought of the security angle." This certainly appeared to be the correct decision to Ira and one that would keep him out of trouble with his boss.

"I'll start the emergency notification call downs now and have my operators start to power down the plant." Marcus hung up the phone and picked up the special red telephone that was a direct link to the NRC emergency operations.

This isn't going to be good right before the election, thought Marcus. The gubernatorial election was only a few weeks away. One candidate, Thomas Conrad, favored nuclear energy, and the other, Allen Rackerby, did not and even endorsed a proposition on the ballot to suspend the use of nuclear energy. One false step by West Isles could sway the public to elect Rackerby. If that happened, all their jobs would be in jeopardy.

Nuclear power plant emergencies have four classifications: Unusual Event, Alert, Site Area Emergency, and General Emergency. The lowest risk classification was an unusual event, which involved a very low-level concern that would not affect plant operation but could possibly cause problems if combined with other failures. The most serious classification, a general emergency, indicated that release of radioactive material to the environment was inevitable and nearby residents to the plant would need to be evacuated. A general emergency had never been declared in the United States; however, the accident at Three Mile Island had come close and was the reason for the creation of the classification system. A security breach where the nuclear safety systems were at risk appeared to fit the classification of an alert, the second of the four levels.

"This is Marcus Laiden, shift supervisor for the West Isles Nuclear Power Plant. I am declaring an alert due to a code C1031 incident, where a security breach of potential safety concern has occurred. This is *not* a drill. I repeat, this is *not* a drill." Marcus had another cigarette in his mouth and lit it as he talked into the receiver cradled on his shoulder.

His first call was to the NRC Emergency Operations Center.

Marcus's next call was linked automatically to FEMA, state and county emergency agencies, and local police. These agencies in turn notified more agencies. Most understood that a security breach was unusual and asked repeatedly if this was a drill. Drills were required on a yearly basis to test the ability of state and federal agencies to respond to an emergency. A real emergency was rare and caught most by surprise. But when they realized the emergency was genuine, all began preparing for the media onslaught.

Chapter 3

LINDY SAT IN THE DECONTAMINATION room in the auxiliary building with Maisie Jones, the on-shift radiation protection technician. The room was down the main hallway from the containment hatch. It had painted concrete walls and a shower stall in one corner. Lindy was sitting in a chair next to a table that had an assortment of supplies: alcohol wipes, Q-tips, gauze, hand soap, and lots of towels. Maisie was slowly going over Lindy's body with a frisker, a radiation detector used to scan for contamination. Maisie watched for deflections on the gauge.

"So, why'd you take your respirator off, Lulu?" Maisie asked. Lindy cringed. She didn't care for the nickname Lulu and wished her friend would drop it. Sure, she acted ditzy sometimes, but "Lulu"? No way.

"Come on, Maisie, I was about to throw up! Who would leave their respirator on in that situation?" said Lindy, still feeling queasy. People usually felt drained after coming out of containment. She glanced at the mirror beside the table. Jeez, she looked more pale and drawn than she feared.

"You're right, nobody would leave it on in that situation," said Maisie.

"Lucky you, though!" continued Maisie. "After this you get to calculate your own internal dose instead of doing someone else's." The calculation of internal dose was a time-consuming project and something Lindy frequently complained about. A person's internal dose is the amount of radiation their body receives from radiation-emitting materials that enter the body. It was hard to explain to people the difference between getting irradiated by a chunk of material sitting outside the body versus having that chunk or particle inside one's body irradiating nearby body tissues. In any event, the NRC requires either type of exposure to be tracked and controlled so that long-term lethal exposures do not occur.

Maisie continued scanning. "Usually in this situation I'd be workin' on some doofy mechanic who thinks all the protections are a bunch of bull and that radiation is actually good for people. It's weird that you're in here. Of course, the mechanic wouldn't have told anyone he'd taken his respirator off, and we would have found he was contaminated at the portal monitor when he was trying to sneak out without detection. You can bet he'd be denying he did anything wrong, and we'd be stuck doing a report on how the contamination got there. At least you fessed up."

"Yep, just call me Honest Abe," Lindy joked.

Maisie slowly passed the frisker back and forth, almost touching Lindy's face with the probe, then moving on to her shoulders. The frisker was the best instrument for measuring small amounts of radioactive material resulting from cross-contamination. Maisie had to do the survey because Lindy could have contaminated herself when she took her mask and respirator off in containment.

"Good news! Your face is not contaminated! Here's a Q-tip," said Maisie, as she handed Lindy the cotton swab.

"Oh joy," said Lindy as she took the swab and wiped the inside of both nostrils. Maisie held a zip-lock bag open, and Lindy dropped the cotton swab in. The Q-tip swab would be used to estimate the amount of radioactive particles she had inhaled.

Maisie was curious about the dead body and said, "You haven't told me any of the details about the body."

Lindy hesitated. "It was the most gruesome thing I've ever seen. Don't want to think about it now ... not recognizable ... and the smell," said Lindy, mumbling as the feeling of nausea returned.

Maisie cringed. "Okay, no need for details." But after a brief period, she could not resist and asked, "Did you find his security badge?"

Everyone entering the plant facility had his or her own security badge with a photo. The badge was also an access card that could open doors where a cardkey was required for entry. Not all badges could open all doors in the plant. Access to high-security areas was limited to the operations staff, the reactor operators, and security staff. Every time a cardkey was used, the security computer made a record of the event.

"No security badge, no dosimetry. Nothing but a rotting body in Tyvek. Funny, the Tyvek looked brand new. It never decays, I guess," said Lindy, almost in a daze. "Ah, yes, Chris checked for dosimetry before we left the minus-10, on orders from the shift supervisor." Dosimetry gear was assigned to each employee entering the controlled area. Being without dosimetry would be highly unusual.

"Any TLD rings?" Coded thermoluminescent dosimeter rings were assigned to one person and therefore useful for identification.

"Are you kidding? Fingers probably decomposed first. It was nasty enough to look for a badge that should have been outside the Tyvek suit. Chris isn't paid enough to dig around inside that suit." She wished Maisie would change the subject.

"Speaking of Chris, how'd it go with him?" asked Maisie.

"Fine. We pretended to be coworkers," Lindy said with finality. Lindy wasn't ready to talk about Chris, even with Maisie. Her feelings were still too raw and also, Lindy feared, uncontrollable.

"Okay, I get it. If you don't want to talk about it, that's fine with me. I thought you might want to. But if you don't, you don't. I know when to shut up."

"Okay, then, shut up!" Lindy snapped. Maisie lowered the frisker and frowned, her brown eyes darkening with displeasure.

"Please," Lindy added with a quick, fragile smile. She knew that Maisie would not take back talk from anyone, especially a friend. Maisie had been raised in one of Philadelphia's tougher black neighborhoods and had learned to take care of herself.

"Okay, consider it dropped," Maisie said, her face brightening with the apology. "Here's another question. Any guesses on who the dead guy is?"

"No. Containment's been buttoned up since start-up last month. Security's probably verifying right now that everyone was out of contaminant after the refueling outage. You know they would check that at every shift change during the outage. It seems unlikely that they will discover anything in the records."

"This is beginning to sound like someone left the body on purpose."

"Yes, looks that way to me, too. This isn't going to be any good for us right before the election." Lindy, too, was worried that if elected, Rackerby would close down the nuclear power plant. Lindy and everyone else would be out on the street if that happened.

Lindy, wearing only her bra and underwear, stood up with her arms out to allow Maisie to scan the rest of her body with the frisker. At five foot eight, Lindy was a couple of inches taller than Maisie. Lindy was thirty-one years old and had a firm, athletic body. Men mostly commented on her long legs. Lindy had dark brown, almost black hair, blue eyes, and ivory skin. The contrasts made for a striking look.

"Did you hear when the cavalry will arrive?" Maisie asked, now bending over to survey Lindy's legs. It was standard procedure to survey the entire body even though the likelihood of finding contamination beyond Lindy's face was slim. A lot of time was spent doing surveys even where no contamination was expected, just to appease the legal department, which occasionally had to defend against claimants who said that working at the plant had caused their cancer.

"Soon. Chris said the NRC had already notified the FBI before we left containment. As for the rest of the cavalry, such as FEMA, the state police, the ANI, INPO, and who knows what others, it will probably be awhile. I'm sure the governor will get involved at some point too; it'll get him on the television. I just hope they figure out what happened and that it's something mundane, like a contractor who accidentally killed himself. It's not beyond the ability of most of the laborers I've run into since working here."

"Yeah, like that guy a few years ago that decided to take a shortcut across a half-built wall in the fuel building and ended up falling several levels and impaling himself on rebar," said Maisie. There were many ways to get seriously hurt as a worker at the plant. Coal mining was one of the few jobs more dangerous than working at a nuclear power plant.

"That was something. Of course, he was lucky to die before the acute rad syndrome got to him. I heard that his wedding ring was so hot from having been activated by the spent fuel stored nearby that they had to send it out as radwaste."

"No way!"

"Yes, way! The company bought his wife a new ring for her to keep. Stable gold is easily activated to gold-198, which puts out a substantial gamma radiation. Rather than stir up any concerns, the company though it best to replace the ring."

"Hadn't heard that before," said Maisie, "although I doubt the ring ever made it to the radwaste building. One of the techs would have grabbed it, not caring about the radiation. Greedy bastards."

"Anyway," continued Lindy, "the only investigation that really counts will be the one done by the American Nuclear Insurers. That's the one that's going to cost us if they find that our security was at fault. High insurance rates could put us out of business." Lindy was aware of all the added costs due to security and safety requirements at the plant. Despite the additional requirements, nuclear power was still competitive in price compared to coal and gas, but that competitiveness could evaporate if costs were to go up dramatically.

"No, Lindy, I think it's going to be the newspapers that will put us out of business. Those antinukes never give up."

"The thought of those reporters having a field day with this situation is making me even more depressed than I was before."

"At least you have good timing on your depression, Lulu," said Maisie, using Lindy's nickname again. "The staff psychologist for the company will be arriving soon. I heard them talking about it at the RP office. I'm sure you'll be first on their list, you being the weak woman and all!" Maisie liked to joke about the chauvinistic attitude common among company workers.

"Oh, great." Lindy was not good at expressing her feelings, even though that appeared to have been a requirement when she met with the psychologist before she was hired. Everyone hired at the plant had to go through a psychological evaluation, which included the Minnesota Multiphasic Personality Inventory and a session with the psychologist once those test results were analyzed.

As Maisie was putting her survey instrument away, the door to the decontamination room opened and Kevin Davenport, another radiation protection technician, stepped inside. He stopped to take a long look at Lindy while she grabbed a towel to cover up.

"Out!" Maisie yelled while she tried to push him back out the door.

"Hey, I'm just following orders! The sup wants to see Andrews in his office," said Davenport, with a big smile on his face, "although I've seen more of Andrews than he ever will."

"Not getting it at home, eh, Thumper? Your wife must be smarter than I thought," said Maisie.

The women workers had to be thick skinned to survive the taunts at West Isles. A quick wit also helped. Some of the men thought the teasing was just for fun, but others used it for leveling—who does she think she is, working at a man's job? Lindy and Maisie were the only two women employed as technical staff in the radiation protection department and the only ones qualified to go beyond the radiation safety control point. A woman working in a technical position had been unheard of a few years ago, but the numbers were increasing every year. During construction of the plant, the engineers had redesigned the restrooms and dressing room to include a women's section, so it appeared that management had finally accepted the inevitable addition of women to the technical workforce. However, there were currently no women reactor operators. Last year the operations department brought in several college graduates to start a training program, but the one woman who applied dropped out early on in the program. The reactor operators took the trainees out on valve line-ups and had them attempt to turn the valves. Some valves were very difficult to turn, even for the strongest operators, so a cheater bar would be used for extra leverage (a cheater bar is a large stainless steel wrench with a three-foot handle). The woman trainee did not have enough strength to turn the valves even with the cheater bar. Since operators have to be able to do valve line-ups by themselves, the woman was disqualified from the job. Some men took this as verification that women were not as qualified as men for any job at the plant.

Kevin Davenport was not like most in that he actually liked having women around. Sex was constantly on his mind, and hence work seemed much more interesting with women around to watch, and even more interesting when occasionally the opportunity arose to cop a feel by accidentally bumping into them. Thumper's reputation was well-known. The women accepted it as one of the prices they had to pay to work at the plant. Lately, however, Thumper rarely succeeded in getting his hands on any women, since new hires were warned about him. He also had a curious habit of sometimes tapping his right foot, and when women were present, his foot tapping would frequently speed up, which is how he acquired the nickname Thumper.

"I'll be there as soon as I take my shower," Lindy replied.

"Okay, but the sup said I needed to stay by you and make sure you are okay," said Thumper, his foot tapping, looking like he was going to make himself at home in the room with a good view of the shower.

"Nice try," said Maisie, and she gave Thumper a big push out the door.

"Hey, quit the pushing," said Thumper, now out in the hallway. "I'm going, but don't be late, Andrews. Maddog is gonna be there."

When the door shut, Maisie said, "I wonder if other jobs have guys this randy."

"I'm sure this is the normal state for many men," Lindy said from the shower, "but if you think about it, how many jobs have as much dressing and undressing as we do? Plus, with the working environment—high stress, dangers, high pressure, a lot of dressing and undressing."

Maisie thought about that. "Makes you wonder about the people who would work here."

Chapter 4

THE MEETING WAS JUST BEGINNING in the control room. The plant manager, Keagan Cahill, also known as Maddog, was a short burly man with russet red hair and blue eyes. He was standing next to an easel that displayed an exploded diagram of the minus-10 level of containment where the corpse was found. The plant manager was a take-no-prisoner's kind and in the past had fired employees on the spot when their job performance wasn't up to par. Cahill's military background clearly influenced his managing style. When he was on site, word spread quickly and any idleness was abandoned.

All the top managers at West Isles were present. The heads of security, radiation protection, emergency preparedness, public relations, maintenance, and operations all stood or sat near Cahill. There were also a few men in suits whom Lindy didn't recognize—probably from the corporate office. Worry was evident on most of the faces.

"I'm sure you are all aware of the importance of handling this situation in the most expedient and professional manner possible. We are going to have national attention because of the discovery of this worker's body and because of the security implications it presents. Those who would like to see this plant shut down are going to use this incident as best they can. So I want all of you to work together in finding out how a body could have gone undetected in containment. The sooner we get West Isles back online making power, the better. I suggest that any of you who have been speed bumps in past situations may want to reconsider that role now. Anyone slowing progress to our goal will be removed by a road crew headed by me. You may want to pass that on to your subordinates also."

Cahill paused and looked around the room. There was a slight shuffling of paper, and most in the room looked down, hoping to avoid eye contact with Cahill. With his volatile temper, even an inadvertent smirk could mean trouble.

"Okay, now I want to hear from each of you on what's been done so far in your department and what you will be doing to resolve this situation." Cahill looked at the operations manager, Mike Dire, who was standing to his left. "Mike, what have you got?"

Mike was tall and thin, with dark red hair and glasses. His fair skin made him seem younger than his forty-five years. He had worked for West Isles since he got out of the navy over ten years ago. He had been the captain of a nuclear submarine. His last four years of service were spent on tour in the western Pacific, several hundred feet under water. Although others appeared nervous and apprehensive, Mike Dire didn't appear phased by the crisis.

As he stepped near the easel, you could see that he still carried himself like an officer: chin high, shoulders back, and stomach in. Mike carried a clipboard that he glanced at as he spoke.

"An alert was declared at 1154 due to a code C1031 security violation. Powering down of the plant began twenty minutes later. Normally an alert classification would not trigger a shutdown, but this particular security violation requires a shutdown if safety equipment is in jeopardy. Since it appears the containment building was accessed without authorization—no one should have been in containment after start-up—we cannot be sure that no harm has been done to any of the accident-related emergency equipment. Emergency notification call down were completed within the fifteen-minute requirement. The NRC emergency operations center, when notified, wanted to know if this was just a drill—they'd never had a security violation emergency condition where it was real and not part of an emergency exercise. The NRC's security team is on its way here. All other calls to state and federal agencies were accomplished without a snag."

"What's the plant status?" asked Cahill.

Mike shuffled through the papers on his clipboard. "Currently we are at 35 percent power—control rod full closure expected at 1930 hours. No problems encountered during power-down so far. Extra operators have been brought in. I've got a crew working with tech support on pulling piping diagrams and system descriptions, looking specifically at emergency systems and equipment in containment, especially anything located on the minus-10 level. That's all I have for now, until we can get into containment and do system walk-downs."

When Mike saw there were no more questions, he moved back to his original location near the wall.

"Harry, you're next," said Cahill.

Harold Clemons, the security manager, was sitting next to Mike. When called, he stood up with some effort, using his hand for leverage on the back of the chair. He was a large man, in his fifties, with gray thinning hair. He was well liked by his staff, although they feared he was going to keel over at any moment from a heart attack. His face was moist from the exertion of standing up.

Harry cleared his throat before he began. "Security level one is now in effect. All high-security areas have been verified secured. Fifty-four plant personnel in the protected area—that is, inside the fence—have been counted and verified as legit. As an extra precaution, the two entrances to containment are being guarded. The FBI has asked that the minus-10 be left as is until their arrival."

Harry paused to catch his breath. Cahill was agitated by the delay. "What do you have on the body?"

"As you know, our security system indicates that no one should have been in containment. Prior to this morning's entry, the last persons in containment were in prior to start-up at the end of the outage. A security guard and an operator made the final entry prior to lockdown to do the security and operations pre-start-up inspection. The body was hidden behind equipment, so it wasn't seen during that inspection. And they didn't note any unusual odors. No one's been in since, according to the security records, so the body must have been there before the end of the outage. As expected, the security records also show that everyone who entered containment for maintenance during the outage also exited at the end of their shift. A security badge was not found on the body ..."

Cahill interrupted, "Who did the search of the body?"

"I did," said Chris Sievers, who was standing behind some staff near the control panels. Lindy was standing next to Chris, and her heart skipped a beat when he spoke. She had almost forgotten about what she had witnessed earlier, but Chris's voice seemed to bring the vision back. She also had fond memories of that commanding voice. She wished they could talk about their relationship and iron things out, but Chris wouldn't even look at her.

As Chris made his way to the front of the room, Harry leaned heavily against the conference table for support. Chris stepped into the inner circle of the managers near Cahill and the easel.

"Tell us all about it, uh, ... what was your name?" Cahill said.

"Chris Sievers, reactor operator." Thankfully, Chris and Cahill's path had never crossed before, so an introduction was needed.

"The body was shoved back behind an electrical panel and some piping over here." Chris pointed to a location on the diagram that showed an electrical symbol, and then he moved his finger to the sump, less than an inch away on the diagram. "This is the location of the sump that registered water, I mean, liquid accumulation. "

"What about the body?"

"Well, at first it looked like someone had stuffed a standard issue Tyvek suit under an electrical panel. When I got closer, I could see there was some bulk inside the Tyvek, and then I spotted the gloves and booties taped to the suit. That's when I pulled on the sleeve, and out came the decomposed head." Chris lost some coloring in his face, but otherwise only briefly stopped. Others in the room grimaced. Lindy looked around the room and wondered who might know more than they were letting on. Lindy noticed that Mike Dire never even batted an eye at hearing Sievers's report. Others looked bothered, even disgusted, but not Mike. He seemed unfazed by the whole thing.

"How odd," Lindy whispered to no one.

"After talking with Laiden at the remote telecommunications station, we went back to the area and looked for a security badge. It wasn't readily visible, so I pulled the suit and contents out of the corner to see if there was a badge underneath or behind it. No sign of a badge. Laiden said to do the minimum disruption, so I didn't look any further."

Cahill thought about that for a few seconds. "Doesn't look good for this to be an accident if a security badge is not with the body. Maybe when the body is removed later, we'll find it inside the suit, if we're lucky."

Nobody held any hope of that, since security protocol required the badge to be visible at all times in the protected area. Besides, any openings in the suit would be taped up before entry into containment. The radiation safety technicians would make sure of that. Couldn't have people getting radioactive dust on their bodies during working hours—it might require staying after shift to decontaminate some poor idiot.

The implications of the missing security badge began to sink in with everyone in the room, but a murder at West Isles just didn't seem possible to anyone, including Lindy. Lindy recalled that there had been tragedy and deaths in the past, but they were always due to the hazardous working conditions. Death by electrocution was not uncommon, considering the abundance of electrical systems and equipment, not to mention the high voltage lines that ran throughout the plant. And then there was the possibility of a deadly superheated steam leak in the turbine building. Superheated steam is invisible and so hot that deep burns occur on contact. Nobody much worried about radiation; in fact, since the high radiation areas where immediate health effects were possible were all locked and inaccessible, it was the least of the safety hazards. West Isles had lost three workers due to accidents during construction and two since the plant came online. Accidental death was not unexpected.

Cahill said, "Thanks, Sievers. Anything else, Harry?"

Harry was now sitting on the table, unable to stand for this long.

"Yes," he said, straightening up. "I've got my computer guys going over the zone entry records for anything unusual since the outage. You know, we had some alarms, but all were resolved as false at the time. But a second look wouldn't hurt. And we've begun compiling a list of all employees, contractors, and visitors who were here during the outage. We are guessing the list will contain about three thousand names. From there, we'll start eliminating names of contacted people. If it becomes necessary, we might be able to identify the person by elimination, but it will take awhile. That's all I have. We'll see if the safeguards people from the NRC have any plans of attack, which I'm sure they will. Costly ones at that, I imagine ..."

"How could a person be left in containment without you guys in security knowing about it?" asked Cahill. Everyone had their ideas, but all waited with anticipation for Harry's response. Harry had made it through the ranks to the security manager because of his adeptness at giving the right answer at the right time. Not only was he a good manager, he was also a very logical thinker. If there was an answer to this question, Harry would be the first to have it.

"Obviously, there are only two ways it could happen, but both seem implausible. One is that the person entered containment without a security badge. During the outage a guard was stationed at both containment entries, and their sole duty was to ensure everyone carded in at the containment card readers. The guard is required to actually check the picture on each badge and insert it into the card reader themselves, so it would be impossible to overlook someone entering without a badge." Harry cracked his knuckles, making Lindy wince. Why did he always do that, she wondered? He was so matter of fact. Did he have to be annoying, too?

Harry continued. "The second scenario appears a little more likely. The person would card-key in, but someone else would bring his security badge out without him. So someone would have to card out twice. Either case would require utter disregard for procedure by the security force, which I'm sure will be covered ad nauseam by the NRC. I probably have at least one short-timer on my staff."

The information seemed to satisfy Cahill for now. As Harry settled back in his chair, Al Jensen, the radiation protection manager, began to speak. Jensen was also an ex-navy nuke who worked on the USS Enterprise, a nuclear aircraft carrier, before coming to West Isles. He was tall, with dark hair and mustache, and usually had a joke to tell.

"At this point, we are waiting to hear what kind of support you all will need for containment entries. If identifying the body becomes an issue, we may be able to help on that front, considering all the records we keep on radiation exposures, rad work permits, etc. Lindy Andrews, over there, will be the lead on getting the NRC, FBI, and other VIPs through radiation safety training and dosimetry badging."

Lindy raised her hand so that everyone would know who Jensen was talking about. This was the first she'd heard that she was going to be playing escort service for the NRC and FBI. The dosimetry technicians who would do the badging could be pretty rude to VIPs. Considering their typical clientele—migrant radiation workers, construction workers, and smart-aleck engineers—they had developed survival techniques that didn't always go over well with the VIPs. Jensen probably thought Lindy would smooth things over so he'd hear fewer complaints. Also, since Lindy used to be a radiation protection instructor at West Isles, she could brief the FBI on how to meet the safety requirements. The NRC people, of course, were already well trained in radiation safety.

"Make sure she has some help," Cahill told Jensen, and then he sat down. Lindy rolled her eyes and fumed. Help? She didn't need any help. That male chauvinist Cahill was an asshole, she thought. She was sick and tired of everyone underestimating her abilities. She would have to prove them wrong. Again.

Other managers talked about press releases, maintenance work to be accomplished while the plant was down, and emergency procedures. The three that Lindy thought were from the corporate office took notes but didn't speak at all. Most of the plant people were tired of talk and ready to get moving. A sense of urgency rippled through the room. Mr. Cahill adjourned the briefing and scheduled another at 0700 the next day.

Everyone began exiting the room, and it took Lindy a minute to catch up with Al Jensen, who was heading to the radiation protection office down the hallway.

"Couldn't you find anybody else to babysit? I've already had a long day," Lindy said, trying to keep up with Jensen's pace and long stride.

"Sorry, Lindy, but you're the only one I trust to keep me out of trouble. I won't be able to brush off complaints from the FBI like I do others that come in about the dosimetry techs." In a low voice, he said, "Maddog is here. Besides, you work with all those women out there and they like you. If I sent any of the RP techs out there as escorts, I would really be in trouble. Dottie and Jane would be in top form after working on the RP techs—primed and ready for the FBI and NRC."

"You're scared of a couple of women?"

"Lindy, you know they need to be on their toes to do their job, but any excesses this time would just cause a lot of trouble that I don't need."

"Okay, I'll do it. So when do the FBI and NRC get here?"

"I heard about eleven tonight, and they want to get going right away. You might want to lie down in the nurses' office to rest for a while. Then can you go over to the dosimetry trailer and get the paperwork started?" Jensen could certainly use the puppy-dog face to get what he wanted. Lindy stopped walking with him since the nurses' office was in the other direction.

"Okay, but I'll remind you of this at my next annual review," she said.

Jensen was walking backward as he talked and almost ran into a technician heading toward Lindy. "You do that. Hopefully, we'll all be employed for next year's performance reviews," he said, and then he turned and walked into the RP office.

Chapter 5

"HELLO?" DOUG DEAVERS HAD TRAINED himself to pick up and speak into the receiver even from a deep sleep. Whether or not he understood what was being said was another thing, but in his line of work half the battle was being ready to go at any hour of the day or night.

"Deavers, I need you here right away," said the voice on the phone.

"Ah, boss? Is that you?"

"Of course it's me. How many calls do you get in the middle of the night?" said Sam Bozworth, the city editor for the *Valley Sun*. "Get your butt in here now!"

The phone went dead.

Doug hung up the receiver and checked the clock near the bed. Almost 11:00 PM. It felt like three in the morning. Without turning on the light, Doug eased himself out of bed and tiptoed to the bathroom to take a quick shower. He didn't see any reason to disturb his girlfriend, Danielle. He quickly got dressed in the suit that was lying on the chair. He brushed his hair and teeth, took a quick look in the mirror, and seeing minimum beard growth, he ran out the door to his car.

There were already several cars in the newspaper's parking lot when he arrived. The production building behind the office was lit up, now printing the next days' newspaper. Doug ran up the stairs and reported to Sam's office.

"What ya got?" he asked, finding Sam staring at his computer terminal.

"It's West Isles," said Sam. Doug raised his eyebrows in response.

"They're powering down—they don't do that for a minor reason. Something about an 'alert' declared. I heard it on the police scanner. Call around. See what you can find out. Start with the company's public relations office. Let me know what you hear."

Doug left Sam's office, wondering what could be happening at West Isles. It could be an important story or nothing at all, depending on the circumstances. Sam had called Doug because he handled the environmental articles for the paper. He covered stories involving West Isles because the environmental advocate groups considered the nuclear plant a serious danger to the environment. Since he found that the technical issues involving the plant were typically out of his league, even one story about nuclear power took quite a bit of time, with all the research required on his part. Recently the utility had sponsored a media day, and Doug had toured the West Isles Nuclear Plant along with fellow media colleagues. The immensity of the facility and technical knowledge behind its operation seemed almost godlike. He found the facility wholly unreal and unbelievable, like something in a sci-fi movie from the 1950s. It was a surprise to him that they used atoms colliding with each other to make power. This scientific feat for creating power using earth's material made him feel small and inadequate. But it did not seem right to take Nature and twist it this way. Ultimately, the tour made him fearful that the mere mortals working in the control room could lose control of the atoms at any moment. He agreed with the environmental advocates that it was too dangerous to have nuclear power plants and found it hard to not let his impressions show in his writing.

Doug searched through his Rolodex for the telephone number of the public relations office at the utility. He had talked with the two public information officers over the last year when he was working on articles related to the upcoming gubernatorial election. A new antinuke governor and the passage of Proposition R—to suspend the production of nuclear energy within three years—would surely shut the doors to West Isles. Doug had heard that the polls were indicating a close vote, and of course this was generating a lot of interest among the public. And what interested the public sold papers.

The line was busy. Figures, thought Doug, probably on the line with other news agencies. He would try later since he would need to get a statement from the utility if there was going to be a story for tomorrow's paper.

Doug thought about whom else he could call and remembered meeting a deputy sheriff when he doing a story on people who lived downwind from the nuclear plant. The deputy sheriff worked at the local station near the plant, so maybe he had information about what was happening at the plant.

"Hello, is Jeff available? No? But is he in?" he asked the receptionist at the sheriff's office.

"Yes, but he is busy manning the emergency desk. You know, there's been an emergency declared at West Isles," said the receptionist.

"Really? An emergency! Did you hear what happened?"

"Yeah, they found a dead guy in one of the buildings. They don't know how the body got there, so the FBI is coming."

"You don't say? Like the federal FBI?" said Doug, playing dumb, hoping she would keep talking. Because its territory covered the rural area around West Isles, this sheriff's office rarely had any interesting activities. The news of a dead body was probably the biggest thing that had happened in the last ten years. It was clear that the deputies never had a problem with information leaks in the past and hadn't thought to tell the receptionist that this was probably information that should not be shared.

"Yeah," she replied, clearly enjoying having someone interested in what she had to say. "I heard that there will be several helicopters coming soon, landing right here at this office. Federal people."

"Wow. Do they know what happened to cause the death?"

"I don't think so. It sounded like nobody was sure who should be called at first. It may be a murder. Can you believe that? A murder right here in Brownsville! It's going to be a first. Hey, I have to go—another call coming in."

"Please give Jeff the message that Doug would like him to call. Thank you." Doug hung up. This could be his night after all! He grabbed his coat and went to Sam's office.

"Boss, it's a murder! They found a dead body in one of the buildings. The FBI is coming by helicopter, so I thought I would head out there and hopefully talk to them after they land."

"You know where they will be landing?"

"Yep. I have an inside source."

"Good job. Okay, I'll call for a cameraman to go with you. Helicopters landing—on the front page—I can see it now!" Sam sat back in his chair, smiling at the ceiling, with his fingertips pressed together in front of him.

Doug put a piece of paper on Sam's desk. "Here's the number of the company's PR office. The line was busy earlier. Can you call and get an official statement for me? Thanks."

After driving for twenty minutes on dark, winding country roads, Doug and the cameraman pulled into the parking lot in front of the sheriff's office, carefully turning off the headlights to avoid notice. There was no sign of a helicopter, a good sign, thought Doug. Three sheriff's cars were in the lot, another sign that the FBI had not arrived yet.

"Quiet, so far. That's good," said Doug. "Hopefully we won't have long to wait."

The cameraman nodded and continued to get his equipment ready, replacing lenses and hooking up a flash unit. It was very dark and there was no moon, so he adjusted the flash for low light. He didn't want the FBI to shoot at him out of surprise from the flash, but at the same time was hoping to get a good shot of them exiting the helicopter.

Doug sat in his seat, biting his nails. This could be the biggest story he'd ever covered, and he didn't want to make any mistakes. In the distance he could see the glow on the skyline in the vicinity of West Isles. Finally, the beating of helicopter blades could be faintly heard. He and the cameraman got out of the car to watch for the helicopter's landing. The four deputy sheriffs who came out of the office building were surprised to see the two of them standing there.

"I'm Doug Deavers, with the *Valley Sun*. Do you mind answering a few questions?" he said, as his cameraman snapped pictures of the officers.

"We don't have a public information officer here right now, but if you wait inside …" said the older officer.

"That's okay. We'll wait out here. I hear there was an accident at the nuclear plant and that radiation is spewing out everywhere? Is that correct?"

"No, no, no such thing is happening. It's just a little security issue. No big deal."

Security issue? It hadn't occurred to Doug that a dead body would be a security issue. This story could get interesting if the body was found in a highly secured area. If the facility can't keep track of their staff, how can they be expected to ensure the safety of the fuel?

"Is your staff trained to go into the plant?"

"No. They don't need to be because the plant has its own security, so if you could just wait. The PIO should be here soon."

"If it was just a murder, wouldn't your office handle it?"

"Now, where'd you hear there was a murder? No more questions. And, please, stay out of the way."

"Could you tell me if the governor is aware of the situation?"

"Of course, of course," said the deputy, appearing distracted by the closeness of the helicopter. He quickly left to meet the helicopter at the pad behind the facility.

As the helicopter landed, the cameraman covered his lenses and waited for the dust to settle. It was clear that the deputy sheriffs were new to this kind of event; they were nervously shifting their weight as they waited for the blades to stop and the occupants to exit.

Two men in dark suits alighted and stood near the helicopter, and the cameraman quickly began taking pictures. The first man to alight walked over and shook the hand of the senior deputy that Doug had been talking to. The flash of the camera interrupted him. Shaking his head, he walked over to Doug and the cameraman.

"Hi, I'm Doug Deavers ..."

"I'm sorry, but we will have no comment." The man appeared to be about thirty-five years old, of average height, and had short wavy blonde hair. He walked with a swagger, commanding attention. "If you have questions, please call this number." The man handed Doug a card and then turned away. "Gentlemen, let's go."

The cameraman took a few more shots as all three sheriff's cars sped off in the direction of West Isles.

"I'm sure I got the shot," said the cameraman.

"Good. Let's get you back to the office and see if we can still make tomorrow's edition." This was going to be an interesting night. Not only did he need to get a statement from the utility, he now also needed a comment from the governor's office. This story was going to sell a lot of newspapers before the election. Doug felt an adrenaline rush and started formulating the article in his head as they drove back to the office. He would have to do some research to see if there had ever been a murder investigation before at a nuclear plant. If not, it could turn into a national news story, and Doug might even see his name on the byline of a story carried in the *New York Times*.

Chapter 6

THE DOSIMETRY OFFICE AT WEST Isles was located in a portable trailer outside the fenced controlled area of the plant. The trailer was situated in the parking lot next to a few other stray trailers used to house extra engineers. Most evenings, the area would be deserted, but not tonight. The lights were on in the dosimetry trailer, and through the windows one could see the dosimetry technicians getting ready for an influx of workers, inspectors, and visitors who would need radiation measuring devices so they could enter the controlled area.

The dosimetry office was responsible for tracking the radiation exposure of all who entered the controlled area at the plant. The NRC required the tracking because exposure to excessive amounts of radiation could be harmful. Current reckoning was that the more radiation that a person was exposed to, the higher the risk of getting cancer. This was based on the health problems encountered by the Japanese survivors of the Hiroshima and Nagasaki atomic weapon explosions at the end of World War II. Some scientists argued that a small amount of radiation exposure was not harmful and possibly even beneficial, but this was controversial among the experts. No data was available for low doses. Rather than risk being wrong, every bit of radiation dose was required to be tracked so that no worker exceeded the amount deemed safe for industrial workers. Radiation doses were measured in rem.

Jane and Dottie looked up from their work when Lindy entered. The room was plain. Filing cabinets lined one wall, and desks with computer terminals were scattered around the room. A small waiting area was created by a counter and a short swinging door that separated it from the work area. The counter was used by people to fill out paperwork, but as far as Dottie and Jane were concerned, it was there to create an air of authority for them, which they gladly took advantage of.

"Hey, Lindy, how you doing?" said Jane, who sat at her desk typing on the computer keyboard. Jane was about fifty, with graying brown hair, brown eyes that could be seen above her reading glasses, and a pleasant round face. Dottie was standing near an open drawer at one of the filing cabinets.

"Not bad considering how my day started," said Lindy.

While Lindy pulled out blank forms, she filled Jane and Dottie in. She covered all the details, the discovery of the body, the meeting earlier with Maddog, and also which VIPs would be coming to West Isles.

"Three men from the FBI should be here shortly," said Lindy.

"You know, I'd rather be snuggling in my bed at home," said Dottie. She, too, was approaching fifty and certainly enjoyed a routine that included a good night's sleep, among other things.

Jane jumped in. "Oh, Dottie! Quit your whining. Think about the overtime you'll be making. Time and a half!"

"I'd rather be sleeping," said Dottie.

"You can sleep tomorrow. Let's make money now," said Jane.

"But I need my beauty rest," said Dottie.

"Well, let me tell you, honey," Jane said with a hand on her hip, "without money, you'll be poor in your old age. No amount of 'beauty sleep' can make up for that."

Lindy laughed. "Good, I'm glad that's settled! Besides, money can buy beauty, so no need to sleep now. Especially since the FBI and NRC will be going into containment tonight. The powers that be have decided it's okay for them to get the extra exposure considering the circumstances. Because of the post-shutdown airborne levels, the three will need to be fitted for respirators. Al wants me to give them the short course on radiation safety—you know, the one that's given during the walk to containment."

"Do you think they'll have any previous rad work history?" Jane asked.

"Hopefully not, since they'll need the full rem limit considering where the body is located," said Lindy.

"Should I get out finger rings? Extremity badges?"

"No extremity badges. Definitely finger rings—not sure what they'll find at the body where their hands will be."

"I'll get the rings ready," Jane said as she went to a cabinet in the back of the trailer.

The door opened, and Harry from security entered with three men in suits and two others dressed casually. Jane and Dottie didn't bother to look up from their desks immediately—no VIP was that important.

Harry did the introductions. "This is Lindy Andrews, who will help you get your radiation protection requirements done. She was also the radiation protection technician that was in containment when the body was found."

Lindy flinched at Harry's words. Hey, she thought, I'm a radiation protection engineer, not a technician! Demoted to a technician already in the eyes of the FBI. Lindy knew that if she was a man, Harry would have remembered she was an engineer with a degree, but since she was a woman, it didn't matter what credentials she had. It wasn't that Harry didn't like her; it's just that in his mind, men were much more competent than women, and really, a woman wasn't smart enough to get an engineering degree. Harry recognized that women had many strengths, but technical ability was not one of them.

Harry pointed toward the three men in suits. "This is Sawyer McMillan, Frank Peters, and Lee Wong from the FBI." The agents nodded at Lindy.

"And this is Sam Scudamore and Tom Johnson from the NRC." They, too, nodded in Lindy's direction.

Lindy looked at Sawyer McMillan. What was it? Was there something familiar about him? No, that wasn't it. He had a crooked nose like he had been in a fight, and he looked like he hadn't shaved in three days. He also had a snooty air about him that Lindy didn't care for. Still, he reminded her of someone. She was sure it was nothing, but like a scientist, she logged the sensory data in for later analysis. "Jane and Dottie here will be helping me with the paperwork to get you dosimetry badges, a whole body count, and fitted for respirators. First, let's start with the paperwork," she said.

McMillan looked a bit agitated by the mention of paperwork and said, "I don't think all this is necessary. We can take care of ourselves in the facility."

Jane looked across the counter and took her first look at McMillan, a long up and down look, then said rather slowly, "Yes, I'm sure you can—take care of yourself, that is."

At this point, one of the NRC inspectors spoke up. "Sorry, McMillan, but no exceptions made on dosimetry paperwork. We can skip the whole body count and respirator fit, I believe. How about that, Ms. Andrews?"

Lindy decided that since this was the first time any of the agents had been at a nuclear facility, it would be okay to skip the whole body count, but the respirator fit would have to be checked when they dressed out in the auxiliary building prior to containment entry. They would also have to sign a waiver saying that they were physically healthy and had had a medical checkup in the last year.

Dottie was standing on the inside of the counter checking Agent Peters' paperwork and recording device numbers. She handed Peters his dosimeter and finger rings, saying, "This TLD you wear on your lanyard, facing out, and also outside your Tyvek suit. The rings are labeled left and right—wear these under your gloves on whatever finger you like."

Looking at the small square black plastic container with a clip on the back, Peters said with some apprehension, although trying to keep it light, "Will I glow after this?"

"Oh yeah, like a lightbulb," said Dottie, and under her breath, not loud enough for Peters to hear, she continued, "Like I haven't heard that one before."

And then Jane, sensing some fun, said, "After this your wife won't need a night-light anymore!"

"Really makes you hot—the radiation. Got to be careful," said Dottie.

"Of course, if you really want to make it interesting, what you need to do while in containment is be sure to ...," began Jane, pausing for effect.

Peters was looking a little concerned, not sure how to take the conversation. Wasn't the Hulk created by too much radiation? Sensing this, Lindy quickly jumped into the conversation and said, "Okay, Mr. Peters and everyone, we are done here, so let's get going."

"But Agent Peters might want to know how to ...," Jane said, in her most sincere, concerned voice, hoping to indicate that Peters was missing out on some important safety information.

"That's okay," interrupted Lindy, "I'll fill him in on what he needs to know." Lindy wasn't sure what Jane was going to say, but she guessed it would be some folklore effect of radiation that was not based on fact.

Jane shrugged her shoulders and looked at Agent Peters with a "too bad I can't help you out" look. Agent Peters appeared concerned, and Lindy knew she would need to do some damage control. As the group exited, Jane and Dottie went back to their desks, smiling to themselves for succeeding in getting a few tweaks on the VIPs.

The cool outside air was refreshing after the stuffy air of the trailer. It was after one o'clock and pitch black except for the lighted plant facility that seemed to hover like a mirage. Lights on high poles were positioned along the security fence and throughout the controlled area, ensuring every location was lit well enough for the security cameras to observe the slightest movement. Straight ahead of the group was the security building, the only access point in or out of the controlled area. The security fence surrounded the entire complex, including the two huge hyperbolic cooling towers that loomed in the distance, dark except for the red safety lights at the top. Grassy fields surrounded the facility, and far off a few lights could be seen coming from farm homes in the area. Lindy would often take walks along the security road, but she especially enjoyed it at night when the loud rasping hiss of a barn owl was often the only sound. The twelve-hour backshift that began at seven at night was always a good opportunity to take the walk, since it took over an hour even at a fast pace and there were fewer people to notice the long absence.

The group received temporary security badges after going through the metal and explosive detectors and having their briefcases put through the X-ray machine. They exited the security building into the controlled fenced area with temporary badges added to their dosimetry lanyard. Lindy led the group, now with the addition of a security escort, providing the basics of radiation safety to the FBI agents as they went. As she walked, she felt a sticky spider web cross her face. Those damned flying spiders, leaving their webs everywhere. She quickly wiped it off her face and wiped her neck, shoulders, and arms to ensure the tiny spider hadn't caught a ride with her. In the spring, it was common to see little cotton-ball wads of web floating through the air and landing randomly on buildings, bushes, cars, and walkways. The spider would be on one long strand, taking his floating cotton puff web for a ride to a new home. It was called ballooning and was a regular practice for many spiders. This season, in particular, the flying spiders seemed to be everywhere, and it always seemed they landed so that the web inconveniently crossed her face.

Lindy was running out of time, so she talked fast and covered only the minimum information. "Since exposure to radiation can be harmful, we track your exposure through your TLD—that little black square piece of plastic around your neck—and by those finger rings you are wearing. We will take them when you exit the controlled area and determine the amount of radiation exposure you had based on what we find on your TLD. You have the maximum radiation limit issued to you—three rem for this quarter. If you exceed that limit, you will not be able to enter any radiation areas for the rest of the quarter—unless a special exemption is made. This is not usually done, so I would suggest you follow the directions given by the RP tech—the radiation protection technician—who will be with you at all times while in containment. He will be carrying a radiation meter, and if he sees that the external radiation levels in the area are too high, he will ask you to leave and go to an area that has a low dose rate. The RP tech has the authority to require you to leave any area if he deems it unsafe." Lindy stopped and put her arms out to stop everyone, and then she looked at the three FBI agents. "This means that you may have to stop your investigation and leave the body immediately? Do you understand this?"

There was some hesitation, but finally they all nodded since they sensed Lindy would not continue until everyone had indicated agreement.

When they reached the auxiliary building, the security guard assisted in ensuring everyone had their card key entered into the card reader at the door. Then Lindy continued. "So, the first safety concern is high radiation areas. The second safety concern is airborne radiation. Since you will be in containment within seventy-two hours after shutdown, the airborne concentrations will be higher than normally found during operation. It will be very important that you keep your respirators on at all times. Inhalation of radioactive material will increase your accumulated dose, which, besides being bad for you, may prevent your entry into radiation areas in the future. Understood?"

Lindy glanced at the three agents, looking for signs of fear, but did not detect anything overt. Peters seemed a little nervous, but that was to be expected for someone entering a new environment. She had found over her years of working in radiation safety that some people had acute radiation phobia. Even some burly mechanics could not work in radiation areas because of the overwhelming fear. Lindy figured it was the years of movies and television shows that had depicted the deadly effects of any amount of radiation exposure. The thought of turning into an inhuman superhero was extremely unsavory to most. The news agencies didn't help either, with their overexaggerated reports of the "lethal effects" of radiation.

"With those warnings aside, I want to remind you that the radiation exposure that you are expected to receive is not lethal—you will not have any adverse health effects from the radiation, except for a very small increase in your chance of getting cancer. And, as always, you all will be safe from overexposure as long as you stay with the RP tech. So don't hesitate to do your job as necessary, within the bounds specified by the tech."

"Lastly, I need to explain the difference between radiation contamination and radiation exposure. Loosely speaking, contamination refers to radioactive particles that can get on your body, the bottom of your shoes, and your protective gear—your Tyvek suit, for example. Once again, it's important to follow the directions of the RP tech when exiting containment and removing your protective gear. We want to leave that contamination on the dirty side of the step-off pad, the dirty side. Also, we don't want you to contaminate yourself when taking off your gear. When you step down onto the clean side of the step-off, you should have left all contamination behind. The step-off pad is an absorbent sticky paper pad taped to the floor and situated at the exit of the contaminated zone. The contaminated zone is roped off and posted with trefoil rad signs and will have fifty-five-gallon drums where you place your respirators and dirty protective gear. Half the step-off pad is in the contaminated zone and the other half is outside in the clean zone. Once you take off your Tyvek and boots, your clean feet should only touch the clean side of the step-off pad. It takes some coordination at first to remove the first booty and have your foot land on the clean side while keeping the dirty booty in the contaminated zone. I suggest you watch others first before attempting your exit."

The three FBI agents listened intently while they walked through the ground floor of the auxiliary building to the elevator. Everyone fit in one elevator, so Lindy continued her talk.

"Most likely you will not come across loose radioactive contamination while in containment. It's kept pretty clean where you'll be. However, you will be exposed to direct gamma radiation from the steam generators and other primary coolant parts, and that exposure will be recorded on your TLD." Lindy again pointed to the badge hanging on her lanyard. "Like an X-ray machine, when you turn it off, the radiation stops, and you are no longer accumulating dose. And once you leave containment, you will no longer be in a radiation field accumulating external dose. And if you keep your respirator on the whole time and carefully disrobe at the step-off pad, you will also be free of any radioactive particles. So, that's your radiation safety short course. Any questions?"

By this time, they had gone down the auxiliary building hallway on the main level to where the locker room was located for donning protective gear. Jerry, a seasoned radiation protection technician, was waiting for them at the RP office just a door down. Al Jensen was smart in having Jerry come in to escort the FBI through containment. He was not afraid to give directions—or, to his mind, orders—to VIPs. The counterintuitive military training that he had received while in the navy had its uses. Usually the military trained the enlisted ranks to obey orders from superiors, but the constant rotation of new officers in the submarine service meant the enlisted men were always more knowledgeable about submarine operations. It was not uncommon for them to disobey orders when the safety of the sailors was at stake.

"Jerry, they'll need their respirator fit test. Just do the banana oil test. And also, on your way in, could you go over how to exit at the step-off pad; it's hard to explain a proper exit without seeing it. And, I'm going home for a few hours." Lindy, having been geared up to do this orientation, suddenly felt drained now that her job was done.

"Good idea, you look like hell," said Jerry.

"Thanks, you always know how to make a girl feel swell," said Lindy as she walked out of the locker room. She took one last look at the FBI agent named McMillan and caught him looking back at her. His sly smile made her uneasy. She didn't like feeling that way.

As she walked down the hall, she could hear Jerry begin his briefing. "Okay, gentlemen, while you dress out, I'll go over the radiation work permit and provide the safety briefing ..."

Chapter 7

MILO PARKER, THIRTY-ONE YEARS OLD with an irksome bald spot, looked in his rearview mirror. "Five cars," he said, talking to himself, "not bad for late evening when rush hour is well over." Milo knew some would think it childish, but it brought him satisfaction to see the frustrated drivers lined up behind him on the single lane road, stuck going slow because of him. Sometimes after work he would go down to Highway 11 just to see if he could beat his record of twenty cars as he traveled exasperatingly below the speed limit. Highway 11 was a particularly enjoyable road to play his game; there were many passing zones, but Milo had impeccable timing and would increase his speed just enough to thwart any attempt to pass him. Of course, after doing that, he was always careful to get off the highway before anyone erupted in road rage.

Tonight, however, the road leading to the lake overlook didn't have any passing broken yellow lines, so the trip was not as entertaining. When Milo reached the overlook entrance, he slowed while still in the lane just to give a little extra pain and remind the other drivers that he was in control. The driver behind him stepped on the gas as soon as Milo was finally off the road.

Milo saw the lone car of his friend at the far end of the overlook parking lot and pulled into a nearby parking space. The friend got out of his car and met Milo at the wooden fence that overlooked Comanche Lake. The sun had already set, and the residual heat of the day was quickly dissipating. Two fishermen were several hundred feet away from the overlook down near the shore, patiently waiting for a bite.

"So, tell me, what happened?" Tom Mietner asked. His eyes shifted back and forth as if scanning for intruders. Tom was what you would call a well-groomed man: tall, thin, well-styled hair, manicured nails, and dressed in an expensive dark suit and tie. The contrast with Milo in his faded jeans and misshapen, stained shirt with an unreadable logo was striking.

"Mr. Mietner, always the one to get right to business," said Milo, "Yes, we've had an unfortunate setback. They've got a little situation at the plant with a dead body."

"A little situation? Are you kidding? This is going to screw everything up! They've called in teams of investigators—no way can you get the job done now!"

"Now hold on a minute, Milo is not a screwup," Milo said adamantly, perturbed by Mietner's tone of voice. Milo had never seen him this upset. When they had first met a year ago, he seemed like such a sincere man, interested in doing what was necessary to get people concerned about the environment and in how Milo could help him in the cause. There had been a sense of camaraderie. Now Mietner was treating Milo just like his father used to.

"No, you're not the screwup. I didn't say that. But what are you going to do when the police come knocking on your door? What are you going to tell them when they ask you what you've been up to, since they are now looking at everything closely? Let's hear it." Mietner was pacing back and forth, one hand rubbing his forehead.

"Okay, okay. Let's not get carried away with the bad news. Better planning in the future is all we need." Milo was now deep in thought, almost oblivious to the presence of Mietner.

"Don't forget we still need that accident that you said you could deliver!" said Mietner. "The polls right now indicate that we are in a dead heat. We could lose the election, and you—you won't get your message out to the people. We both lose unless you can come through, despite the current mess."

"Yes, I agree. The people need to hear Milo's message," said Milo in a far-off voice.

Milo was suspicious of electricity. Even at a young age he sensed the effects of what he later learned was the electrical field created around electrical sources and appliances. When he got to school, he learned that the industrial revolution had brought electricity closer to humans, whereas human contact with electrical fields was rare before then. Milo knew that electric fields were very dangerous to people and the environment. There was a subtle effect on the human cell. He had read in the magazine *Science* that laboratory research had shown this to be true. Scientists had designed tests that showed observable changes to cells in the presence of intense electrical fields. The cells did not die, but the internal parts appeared to change locations and line up parallel to the field. After the field was turned off, the cell seemed to return to a normal state and survive at the same rate as other cells that were not exposed. Although the scientists did not confirm this, he believed that the cells in his body were, in a sense, being attacked and somehow handicapped by electromagnetic waves when he was in a field. He felt his cells were under stress in the presence of electric fields and that they were not able to perform their appointed functions. In sixth grade he purchased an electromagnetic field detector from an army/navy surplus store and began to test his environment to see if it was true what he was sensing. And sure enough, whenever he measured EMF on his meter, he could feel the stress to his cells. There were small electric fields around all the appliances in the kitchen as well as around the air conditioner and the television.

Milo tried to tell his father about his discovery and how dangerous it was for him to sit in front of the television every night, but his father thought he was being preposterous and made fun of his fear. On one occasion, his father had Milo sit in front of the television, and while laughing at Milo's discomfort, he said, "See? What'd I'd tell you? You're not burning up! Look, nothing's happening to you! Now stop being an idiot and get out of my way—you're blocking my view."

Milo learned that it was best to keep his discovery a secret. He did not share his knowledge with anyone for the longest time. But he made sure to limit his exposure to EMF. To prevent the need to carry around his EMF detector all the time, he mapped out the EMF fields near every place he went during the day to determine where it was safe to be. It had been a challenge to map the West Isles plant, but he had accomplished it on backshift when there were fewer people around. When required, he could maneuver around the unseen electric fields in such a way that others could not notice what he was doing. He rarely walked in a straight line from one location to the next. He never went to the turbine building when the plant was producing power; the EMF was strong and the field large due to the immense size of the motors. Milo had added shielding to his car to prevent exposure while he was driving. Milo could not comprehend how everybody did not sense what their own cells were experiencing. It saddened him to see the slow death people were unwittingly suffering due to their ignorance, but at the same time, he felt superior to everyone because of his special knowledge.

A few years ago Milo attended a meeting of the environmental group, People for a Safe World, where he felt comfortable in sharing his knowledge. They found his theories unusual but listened to him intently and did not ridicule him. People for a Safe World had its own theories that were not accepted by most people, so philosophically Milo fit in. At last he had found others like him who cared about people and had vision; and People for a Safe World found someone whose fanaticism would be useful for their purposes. People for a Safe World had purposely worked to position people in key positions at facilities, such as at nuclear power plants, which they adamantly opposed. Milo had been at the power plant for several years and was finally called to duty this past year. His friends in People for a Safe World had introduced him to Mietner.

"So, Milo, what can you do?" Mietner said. The man was in his face. Milo could smell his cologne. It was one that more sophisticated men used.

"Uh," Milo said slowly as he shook off his thoughts and returned to the conversation, "Milo will need to work on it, uh, yes, work on another plan. Let's see, we'll need to wait until things cool down a bit at the plant. There's still time before the election to let that happen. And there are still a few things Milo needs to fix in the containment building ..."

"As we discussed before, you really need to cause a bad accident at the plant, like a meltdown where there is radiation released to the environment. Can you still do that?"

"A meltdown you're not going to get, like I said before. There are just too many backups and safety systems and checks and balances. You know, the plant is really pretty safe, so a venting of rad gas is all you're going to get. The LOCA is still the best option ..."

"Low cah?"

"LOCA is short for loss of coolant accident. You know what that is, don't you? Heard of the China syndrome?" Mietner nodded in

41

agreement, and Milo continued. "A LOCA would be most desirable, but the backup safety systems would kick in before the supposed China syndrome could happen. Although, now that the body has been discovered, I doubt that I'll have the access or the laziness of the security staff at my disposal like before. Security is going to get hit hard during the investigation and won't be so lax in the future."

"But you will be able to do something, right?"

Milo enjoyed the neediness in Mietner's voice and being in control once again. Not so powerful now in your fancy suit and styled hair, isn't that right, Mr. GQ? Should Milo let him pass or continue to dominate him?

"Oh, yeah, I'll think of something," Milo said, deciding to let Mietner pass. "I'll call when I have a plan worked out."

On the drive home, Milo thought about the different options he would have for causing an accident at the facility. His original plan was to plant some radioactive iodine in the containment building ventilation system and have it leak out into the environment and cause the public to be exposed. A friend of his was supposed to get the radioactive iodine for him. But now with the heightened scrutiny, this plan was undoable. Milo had to come up with a new plan to cause a problem at the plant, and this was going to take some time. While in a systems training class, Milo had learned about the backups to the backups and the multiple redundant safety features around the plant. It was beyond Milo to know how to create an actual release of radioactivity from the reactor; however, Milo knew that a solution would come to him, because his mission was important to humanity.

*   *   *   *

Inside the Rackerby for Governor campaign headquarters, Greg Montague sat in a high-backed chair and said, "I talked with my guy, and it looks like we will have some help on the nuclear issue before election day."

"Good," Rackerby said, twiddling his pen. "I was looking at the latest tracking polls, and we're losing ground. We need a bump."

"What I'm expecting is something that will guarantee you a big bump right into the governor's office," said Montague, looking at his fingernails and acting very comfortable with the discussion.

Rackerby grinned.

"You are one tough dude, Montague," the candidate said. He leaned back in his plush leather chair and pointed his pen at Montague. "When I'm elected, I'll find a place for you in the capital. I promise."

"That's all I want, boss. All I want. Of course, it'd better be a good job since I will owe some favors," Montague said and got up from his chair, turned, and left.

Chapter 8

WHEN PEOPLE FLICK THE LIGHT switch in their home, the technological achievement that has to occur to allow that bulb to light up is usually beyond their comprehension. If asked, most would have no idea how the electricity was generated that allowed them to turn on that light. They know that a power plant is needed, but not why and how the power was made that allows light at the flip of a switch. On the other hand, people have no trouble answering the question of where this power plant should be located: anywhere except my backyard, my town, my nature preserve. Now if that lightbulb did not light up when needed, then there was going to be hell to pay, because electricity is a basic human right, isn't it?

At West Isles, the radiation protection office was like the home kitchen: everyone congregated there. Today was no different. The office was located off the main hallway of the auxiliary building between the control room entrance and the locker room near the control point entrance leading to the containment building. The office was similar to other spaces in the auxiliary building in that it had no windows, no decorations beyond a chart of the nuclides and a few memos taped to the walls. The desks and filing cabinets were surrounded by painted concrete walls. Several chairs were available, since this was where briefings took place.

Prior to any work in the controlled area, a meeting was held to go over safety concerns and to walk through the work plan. Every job had a briefing, but only those involving a high radiation area or other industrial hazard were taken seriously. It was helpful to go over the steps required for a job ahead of time, because that allowed them to streamline their motions and thereby reduce time in the radiation areas. For the more involved jobs, a mock-up would be constructed of the piping and other structures involved in the job so that the steps could be practiced. There was a building on site that stored all the mockups made for practicing repairs, such as wooden platforms with thirty-inch pipes simulating a reactor coolant hot leg. The hot leg is the section of the primary reactor system that delivers superheated water to the steam generator. It is one of the more radioactive components, since it carries water that has been in close contact with the fuel, and it requires close inspections periodically to ensure its integrity.

It was around lunchtime, so workers were already starting to assemble prior to the break. Thumper and Jack Huston, another radiation protection technician, occupied two of the chairs in the office. Jack Huston was in his forties but looked much older because of the ruggedness of his face. He had light brown hair that was thinning on top. He was smoking a cigarette and drinking his coffee, listening to Thumper.

"Listen to this," Thumper said loudly from his chair in the corner, newspaper hiding his face, "the FBI has not been able to identify the body found in the containment building, but they do say they have several leads. Yeah, right. They don't have squat. Yet they still make it sound like they've got something to investigate to the press."

Cal Sherwood, radiation protection shift supervisor, didn't bother to look up from his paperwork. He was in his late thirties and had worked at West Isles for about ten years. Before that, he had put in six years in the navy as an engineering laboratory technician on a submarine. He knew his stuff. "And your point is?" he asked, "You've been known to make a bad situation downright pretty when your butt was on the line. What'd you expect the FBI to say?"

"Hey, I'm just pointing out that you can't believe anything you read in the paper," said Thumper, looking at Jack for support.

"Damn right. And it took you how long to figure that out, Thumper?" said Jack.

"Well, at least the pictures for the article are good. Did you see the one of the FBI getting off the helicopter? Nice lighting. See here," Thumper said, leaning over to show Jack. "I especially like the picture of the FBI shaking the hand of the deputy sheriff. It has all the pretentiousness of an official meeting, like heads of state meeting."

Just then, the new junior radiation protection technician, Daryl Farnsworth, burst into the office and said, "Guess what? On the walk-down of the aux building with the feds, they found a bed! With sheets and candles and everything. They're calling in the fingerprint guys to collect samples."

A walk-down is where every section of pipe and component of a particular system is visually checked for integrity and alignment. There are about hundred individual systems at West Isles; luckily, only the systems associated with the reactor coolant system required a walk-down.

Cal and Thumper briefly glanced at each other, wondering how this would play out. It was common knowledge that Karen North and John Carlyle had been doing it somewhere during work hours, but nobody had known where. Since they were both married, it appeared it worked best for them to take breaks together at work. Daryl Farnsworth was the young new hire and wasn't in the know, so better to keep it that way for now while the FBI was checking things out.

"Really? Wow. Daryl, you mean, like someone was sleeping on the job?" said Thumper.

"Uh, yeah, but maybe more like …," Daryl said, now sounding unsure of himself. With a tilt of his head he removed his rather long red hair out of his eyes, his freckled face turning slightly pink from embarrassment.

"Like someone was living in the aux building? Free rent?" said Jack.

"Well, maybe that … that was the case, but …" Daryl was now very unsure of himself and stammering.

"Where was it?" asked Thumper.

"Minus-30 behind the east fan cooler. There was insulation pads stacked on the floor."

"You think people were doing it there? Nobody would be that stupid," said Thumper.

Surprised by the negative response and lack of apparent interest, Daryl left, wondering if he had overreacted to the news.

"That kid is gullible. Has a lot to learn about working here," said Cal.

"Aw, he'll be fine. He reminds me of Opie on the Andy Griffith show. That's it! From now on, I'm calling him Opie," said Thumper. It was part of the breaking in for the new guys to get a nickname. Once they'd been around awhile, people would revert to referring to Daryl by his last name.

"Hey, did you hear about Andrews and Sievers calling it quits? Ingalls was telling me he saw Chris moving boxes out of Lindy's house. You had to notice Ingalls was taking the day shift lately—when Andrews is at work." Thumper kept up with all the relationships and gossip of the plant. He had his own title for his daily reports: As The Turbine Turns.

"Ingalls doesn't have a chance," said Jack.

Two men entered the office, their hair wet and still sticking to their foreheads due to the hardhats they had just taken off. They carried clipboards and meters with probes connected by a cable. They dropped the gear on the desks and then sat in the nearest chairs. Homemade duct tape straps hung from the probes.

"It seems hotter out there in the tank farm. Must be due to heat deflecting off the metal tanks," said Billy Kilroy, the older technician. Billy had beard stubble that was graying, and he walked with a distinct limp.

"Anything unusual?" Cal asked.

"Nope, same background numbers as all the hundred other surveys done in the tank farm. Go figure," said Kilroy. These routine surveys rarely uncovered anything, but on the very remote possibility that there would someday be a leak from one of the tanks, they would need to address it immediately. Surveys were done even though the tanks were inspected annually and any signs of erosion were repaired as soon as possible, preventing the likelihood of a leak in the first place. The drudgery of these types of surveys wore on the technicians after a while, and most tried their hardest to avoid the job.

"Did you use your best girlie handwriting like I asked? The FBI and NRC are looking at every survey report. They keep complaining that you techs can't write or spell and that maybe we should send you back to kindergarten," said Cal.

Kilroy took a couple of sheets of paper off the clipboard and gave them to Cal. "Here, Cal, check for yourself."

Cal set the papers aside with hardly a glance and picked up another from his desk. Meanwhile, Thumper got up from his chair and handed Kilroy a pink slip of paper that had "Telephone Message" printed at the top and a handwritten message in the lined section.

He looked at the message for a minute and said, "Who took this message? I can't read it! I think it's from my wife, but most of the writing is unreadable."

And then, after a closer look at the note, he said, "Uh, excuse me, I have a phone call to make."

Thumper snickered after Kilroy left the room, and the others looked at him questioningly.

Thumper said, laughing harder as he spoke, "What? I didn't do anything!"

Sensing that nobody was buying his noninvolvement, he continued, "All right, I made up a phone message from his wife. That's all. Of course, the note was illegible, except for a couple of words, like 'it's over' and 'divorce.' No big deal."

The others in the room chuckled. Cal shook his head in disbelief.

Cal said, "Thumper, obviously you have too much spare time on your hands. Engineering has a job to do as soon as the can is unbuttoned. It's a pretty high contamination area, so we will probably need two techs." The "can" was slang for the containment building, possibly because the shape of some containment buildings was similar to a can. The containment building at West Isles had a domed top.

"I'll do it," said Milo Parker, the other technician who had returned from the tank farm with Kilroy. "Anything besides contamination surveys. Where in the can is the job?"

"Uh, it says here, the minus-20. Replace a flange on the number 4 safety injection pump," said Cal, looking at the paperwork.

"Sounds good to me," replied Parker, sounding casual, although Jack looked at him with a questioning look, noting the change is his normal oddball behavior.

At that moment Lindy walked through the door, and Jack watched as she moved directly to Cal.

"Cal, ops wants a tech right after lunch to escort another group of FBI into containment to retrieve the body. Also, you will need extras at step-off to help with surveying the body out. Who you got?"

Thumper jumped in quickly and said, "Hey, Andrews, this sounds like a job made just for you. Heard you were looking for a new man— and lucky you, this one in containment can't run away from you."

Rumors had already circulated that Lindy fainted after the gagging episode when she encountered the body yesterday. Some found that very entertaining, along with the fact that she had just broken up with Chris. On top of that, everyone just assumed that she was looking for a new man, even though it wasn't true.

Lindy showed no sign that she heard the comment and continued directly with Cal. "Any of your peons will do. It's gotten around about what the backshift techs did to that FBI agent—lucky for them the agent didn't complain to Jensen. In the future, I would keep your serfs on a short leash. Wouldn't want Maddog to hear about their antics—by accident—while I loudly talk about the incident in the control room." She left, heading to the nursing station located down the hall.

Thumper registered Lindy's subtle threat and thought in the future it might be best to be a little more restrained with her. However, the mention of antics on the backshift had peaked Thumper's curiosity. "What happened on backshift? What'd I miss?"

Cal had heard all about it at shift turnover that morning. "It was classic Jerry. He had taken the first group of FBI and NRC guys into containment early this morning. I guess he was on his best behavior for most of the job, until they all left through the hatch and were in the exit area near the step-off pad. The one FBI agent named Peters seemed pretty nervous about getting his gear off without contaminating himself. While trying to step out of his suit, he fell down and used his bare hands to break his fall. The floor in the exit area was slightly contaminated where he touched it, so when Jerry frisked his hands, some contamination was found. Jerry had the meter turned down to lowest scale."

Everyone nodded in understanding, knowing that on the lowest scale the meter would already be clicking away solely from the normal background radiation, so even a small amount of contamination on the agent's hand would sound significant. Most technicians worked using the next higher scale so that the background clicks were less frequent. On the lowest setting, the slightest increase would sound like the meter was going off scale to the inexperienced and that lethal levels were being detected.

"Instead of just cleaning the guy's hand, Jerry jumped back, as if the rad level was so high he needed to back away. Then Jerry proceeded to go through all the drawers and cabinets on the decon cart, pretending to look for something. After that he got on the phone with engineering and asked where the steel wire brush was—that he had to decon a guy and couldn't locate it. Peters was standing there the whole time with just his skivvies on and his suit down around his knees, looking pretty nervous. Peters asked Jerry if the wire brush was really necessary."

"What'd Jerry tell him?" asked Jack, enjoying where this was heading.

"Jerry replied, 'Just relax, the wire brush doesn't really hurt that bad.' Jerry proceeded to tell Peters that if he continued to get nervous and sweat that the contamination would go deeper and take more scrubbing to get out; maybe even a layer of skin would need to be removed."

At this, Jack and the others were laughing pretty hard, imagining that nervous FBI agent standing there in his underwear, wondering if the technician was going to do a "Silkwood" on him. Most workers at power plants found the movie *Silkwood* generally ridiculous. No one would even consider using a wire brush to decon a person. The abrasive action would only drive the contamination deeper. If there was anything the public could not forget about that movie, though, it was that scene where they deconned Silkwood with a wire brush. Unfortunately, it appeared that the movie had actually swayed some in the public against nuclear power, even though the story was about a nuclear weapons factory.

Cal continued. "Knowing Jerry, he probably would've kept on going with the gag, but luckily Giltner who was on the backshift with Jerry came by to help out. He had Peters wash his hands, and of course the contamination was removed."

"Wish I had been there," said Thumper, almost dreamily. "I would have found a wire brush for Jerry."

"Okay, everybody," said Cal, looking at his watch, "get to lunch, and when you return, we will have the afternoon work permits ready for you." Cal turned back to his desk to start the paperwork.

"Hey," said Vinnie Balluchi, a reactor operator who was now standing in the radiation protection office doorway. "Has anybody seen a cheater bar lying around? We've seemed to have misplaced one." All the technicians shook their heads. "Well, if you happen to run across it, let me know." And then Vinnie was gone.

Chapter 9

LINDY OPENED THE DOOR TO the nurses' office located down the hall from the radiation protection office. Inside sat Sawyer McMillan behind a desk and surrounded by boxes filled with computer printouts. The room had that antiseptic smell often present in doctor's offices. There was a cot sitting near the medical cabinet with a pillow and blanket. It looked like one of the cots that the company kept in storage at the emergency operation center of the plant. McMillan looked up and waved Lindy to the chair across the desk from him.

"Ms. Andrews, thank you for coming to this interview," he said. "I hope you've had a chance to get some rest since the last time I saw you."

"Yes, I have. Thank you." Lindy saw that McMillan was now wearing reading glasses, which made him appear even more condescending.

"Good. As you know, we've been interviewing all workers at the plant, and those who had access to the power building are of interest to us. Do you know when you were in the power building last? That is, before the time you went in when the reactor was turned on?"

"Ah, do you mean my last entry into the containment building before I made the power entry?" said Lindy, making sure she understood the question. Entries into containment when the reactor was producing power were called power entries. McMillan nodded. "I could check my records to be sure of the exact date, but it was a few days before the spring outage was over."

"No need to check records," said McMillan, looking down at a computer printout, "the security record says you entered on May 23 at 0821 and exited at 1049. Is that correct?"

Good God, Lindy thought, exasperated. If he already knew when I was in there, why did he bother to ask? Is he trying to trick me?

"Yes, sounds about right."

"What was the purpose of the visit?"

"There was a welding job going on that I wanted to observe. It was on one of the radiation monitors located in containment. I wanted to get a good look at the final monitor orientation after the welding was done ..."

"Orientation? What do you mean?"

"I mean how the radiation monitor was mounted and how the probe face was positioned—whether it would be facing straight out, down, or oriented more toward the dome of containment. This monitor is used to calculate radiation concentrations in the air in containment, in case there is a leak. It would probably give a different reading if aimed up."

"I see," said McMillan, not looking at her. He took his time before asking the next question.

"Too much information?" said Lindy, noting that he was still writing.

"No, not at all. Just a bit hard to keep up with all the instrumentation around here and the terminology. What else did you do in the power building?"

"In containment," Lindy emphasized the word, "I toured all accessible areas—always good to take the opportunity to look around and remind myself of the location of equipment. I went down to the minus-40 level and back up to the plus-20 to check out another monitor."

"Something you always do? Take a tour?"

"Well, yes, I try to when I have time. It could be eighteen months or more before containment is opened up again. Usually these reactors just hum away until the fuel runs out."

"And did you notice anything unusual during your tour?" McMillan said. Lindy sensed a bit of sarcasm in his voice, as if he didn't believe a tour was necessary. At this point Lindy was feeling that the interview wasn't going very well. Others had discussed getting a lawyer just in case the blame went their way.

"No, nothing unusual."

"Do you have any idea who the victim could be?"

"No."

"Do you know of anyone who has threatened another person here at the plant?"

"Well, there was the time that two engineers went at it in a meeting. One had accused the other of being incompetent, and the discussion got pretty heated. And afterward the two were fighting in the hallway until the shift sup came and broke it up. That was about two years ago. A pump had been installed backward and caused an unexpected SCRAM, which delayed start-up for about a week. Expensive mistake."

"Heard about that—the engineers will both be interviewed once we find the one that was fired. What's a SCRAM?" asked McMillan.

She had used that word for so many years in talking to other workers that it hadn't occurred to her that it would be foreign to anyone. It reminded her that she needed to get out more and hang with normal people once in a while.

"SCRAM is an acronym for 'safety control rod axe man.' It's an old acronym ..."

"What? No axe men working at West Isles these days?" said McMillan. Lindy noted this was the first hint that McMillan had a sense of humor.

"Right. In the old days they had to improvise. In 1942 or so, Fermi, you know, one of the nuclear physicists who later worked on the Manhattan Project?" McMillan nodded. "Well, Fermi created the first uranium 'pile' and had a man with an axe standing on scaffolding overlooking the makeshift reactor that Fermi and his crew had built under the stands at Stagg Field at the University of Chicago. The axe man stood by the rope that held up the cadmium control rod and was ready to chop the rope if Fermi asked. Cutting the rope would drop the control rod, and that would halt any chain reaction. But really, I think Fermi called the man the safety control rod 'action' man, but 'axe' has a much better ring to it. Nowadays the term SCRAM is used loosely for the instantaneous automatic insertion of the control rods to their full position so that shutdown of the chain reaction occurs immediately. By the way, a SCRAM is not the preferred way to shut down, since it causes a jolt to the reactor coolant system, and then inspection is required."

"Thanks for the clarification," said McMillan as he continued to write. "Now, how about your personal relationships? And, also, do you know of any coworkers having relations?" asked McMillan, now looking straight into Lindy's eyes. His funny-looking spectacles didn't hide the fact that he had eyes the color of the Caribbean.

"My personal relationships? I mean, everyone knows about Karen and Carlyle," Lindy said, not really interested in explaining her current situation with Chris.

"We will be interviewing Karen North and John Carlyle. But yes, your personal relationships. Are you involved with anyone?"

"Um, I'm single—newly single—not seeing anyone." Lindy tried her hardest not to sound sniveling. "Chris Sievers and I recently broke up, but there are no hard feelings. Things just didn't work ..."

"Fine. Okay, so what is your job here, and where have you worked before?"

"I'm a radiological engineer, currently acting as the dosimetry supervisor until they hire a replacement. Prior to that I wrote procedures and reports on dosimetry data, especially when there was a high or unusual reading recorded that required research. Basically, I do anything my boss, Al Jensen, needs me to work on in support of keeping the plant operating," Lindy said, emphasizing the last line using her official voice. It was a line everyone used when they needed to justify their work. Sensing little reaction from McMillan beyond his frantic scribbling, she continued. "I worked for a while as a contractor, doing rent-a-tech work at outages at other plants before coming here. Before that, I was a student at Colorado State University in the health physics program."

"What other atomic plants did you work at?"

"When I graduated, I went to work for a while with a contract firm at the Three Mile Island plant, you know, the power plant that had the accident? Then I went to Florida to work on an outage at Crystal River. After that, I worked for a while at the Rocky Flats plant, but I didn't like that much. Then I got hired here. Been here for two years. Want more detail?"

"No that's good." McMillan looked at his watch, stood up, and said, "That's it for now. I have another interview shortly. You can go now. Thank you for your time."

"You're welcome."

Lindy got up from the chair and was about to reach for the doorknob when McMillan said, "Do you have any plans for dinner tonight?"

Her hand froze. Holy crap. What did he say?

"Uh, excuse me," she stammered, turning back to face him. "I wasn't listening. Did you ask me something?"

"Yes," McMillan said as he removed those silly reading glasses, "I wondered if you had dinner plans. I need a break from this place and don't know of any nearby restaurants that have decent food. And I have a lot of questions about radiation and atomic plants but don't have time now to talk. If you don't mind answering questions during dinner, that will allow me to get out but still get some work done."

"Ah, sure, I guess that would be okay. But isn't it wrong to be fraternizing with the suspect? Isn't there some FBI rule against that?"

"That's true, but I've already taken you off the list."

"I see. Sure, I can get you some decent food not too far from here. Meet me in the dosimetry trailer when you are ready?"

"I will be there," said McMillan, and he turned back to his paperwork.

You fool! She chided herself as she walked down the hall. She wondered why she had agreed to have dinner with that arrogant bastard. Yes, he was arrogant.

Chapter 10

McMillan followed Lindy in her truck down the winding country road to the small town of Brownsville and to a small building located several blocks from Main Street. Lindy got out of her truck and waited for McMillan to park.

She asked, "Far enough off the beaten path?"

McMillan stood in the gravel parking lot and looked up at the old building that housed Mamacitas. "Yes, I think so—it looks too rustic for reporters."

The interior of Mamacitas was sparsely lit by candles and dusty overhead lights covered in oriental paper shades. On the walls were paintings done on black velvet, and handmade pottery of various sizes lined the windowsills and shelves. There were only a couple of tables occupied by what looked like painters or construction workers having a few cervezas with their dinner. McMillan and Lindy sat down on the other side of the room from them.

"You made it past the reporters at the gate without incident," said Lindy. "They didn't seem to notice you. I thought they would stand in front of your car to get an interview! It's been a slow news day. I heard they were trying to interview anybody entering or leaving the plant."

The two local papers and three TV news stations had posted staff at the gate with cameras ready in case there was any breaking news about the mysterious death.

McMillan swigged the cola that the waitress had brought him.

"I guess you get a lot of press coverage anyway," he commented.

"Brother, you don't know the half of it," Lindy said as she munched on a chip. "Those nutty People for a Safe World are always trying to shut us down."

"Who?"

"People for a Safe World," Lindy explained. "When the plant was under construction, they organized protests and tried getting into the protected area by climbing the fence. One almost made it, but an officer finally got him down and hauled him off. The press had a field day."

"I remember seeing that on the news," nodded McMillan. "How long did it go on for?"

"Oh, I guess about a year. In spite of all the negative coverage, the plant eventually received an operating license. The protesters continued to maintain a presence at the facility gate, but as the plant ran day after day without incident, they slowly disappeared. The news agencies also moved on to other stories. But now with this proposition on the ballot to shut down West Isles, I guess we are newsworthy again."

McMillan shrugged. "Well, I'm glad none of the press hounds recognized me."

"Good thing—you wouldn't look so hot on TV right now. Doesn't the FBI let you sleep?"

"Sometimes. I'll sleep tonight. Not to worry. I will admit, that cot in the nursing station is looking better and better!"

This was the first time Lindy had seen him smile. It was nice to see that it might not be all business as it had been earlier at her interview.

The waiter came, and they ordered their food. McMillan also put in orders for his coworkers who were at the plant continuing with interviews. Lindy was feeling a little tense with an FBI agent sitting across from her. She tried not to look at him too much even though she was drawn to observing his movements. Sawyer had a strong face with an angular jaw and a roman nose. His blue eyes revealed very little. His blonde hair was short, but not military short. Lindy had noticed previously that he was very comfortable with his body, stood straight, and walked with confidence—obviously an ex-military guy. He still seemed arrogant, though. Lindy sipped her tea.

McMillan opened the notebook he was carrying and tapped his pen on the page.

"Thanks again for helping me out here. This is beginning to look like a murder, and I find I'm way behind the curve on understanding all the angles with all the intricacies of the atomic power business. It has its own language."

"Yes, I guess it is like its own language! It should have a name, you know, like nukespeak, or maybe nuc-monics?"

"Not bad. Nukespeak works for me. The acronyms and buzzwords are constant with you all. And I've got to say, you've got some rather unusual coworkers. Is there something about West Isles that everyone's not telling me? I mean, are all atomic power plant workers like this? Moreover, and beyond the quirkiness, there's this no-holds-barred approach and a know-it-all attitude, and I have yet to get the same opinion from any two people."

"What? Are you thinking that radiation makes the workers act 'unusual'? Strange people are everywhere and so is radiation, so you can't blame nuclear power." Lindy had been through this same conversation about radiation with many people, and no matter what she said, people's minds were not changed and they kept their irrational fears.

"West Isles workers are unusual, but not because of the radiation. It takes a certain personality to survive at a power plant. The company loses about half a million dollars in revenue every day that the plant is not running. On days when electrical power is in short supply, whether the plant is operating becomes a safety issue, especially during the summer when high temperatures can be lethal for the elderly. The utility likes to have the nuclear plant as the steady base power source, turning on the more expensive natural gas power plants as demand increases. Remember, power can't be stored, at least cheaply, so there have to be enough power plants to cover the peak demand. There is a lot of pressure to do the job right and at the same time get back online as soon as possible after outages and unexpected power-downs. Outages are usually strategically planned to coincide with low power usage in the springtime. It's almost like every minute counts when the plant is down and time is wasting. And that's just one aspect of the job. There are also the inspections during the slow time when the plant is running. We get regular inspections by the NRC where they come in and look at just about every record, checking every detail to see if any procedure was violated so they can issue a fine. When they aren't here, the American Nuclear Insurers come in and do it all over again. Do you have somebody coming in and checking every piece of paper you generate in your office? No? And did you know there's a department at West Isles that just does safety and quality assurance inspections? We can get written up by that group too. We also have security staff constantly monitoring security violations like tailgating and propping open a security door. You get points for each violation—too many and you are out the door. And did you know, also, that many plant staff expend about a quarter of their time in training so they can maintain their qualifications? Fail a test and you lose your job. Oh, lest I forget, there's our favorite requirement—the fitness for duty requirement requiring yearly and random drug and alcohol testing. Why there's …"

"Okay, okay, I got it. Sounds like it's a tough place to work." McMillan could tell that Lindy was just reaching her stride and probably could talk nonstop on the subject. In a way, it was refreshing to find a woman who was passionate about something other than the latest fashion trend.

"And by the way, just so you know, no one calls it 'atomic' power anymore. That went out in the 50s. You keep calling it the 'atomic power plant,' which sounds so old-fashioned."

McMillan laughed goodheartedly about being lectured to by this woman and was wondering if maybe fashion subjects would be easier. Sometimes it hurts to get what you wish for.

"Thank you for lesson number one," said McMillan as he looked at his notepad, ready to get back to business. McMillan pulled out his reading glasses and put them on. This time, Lindy thought, the glasses made him look scholarly.

"Now, let me get back to what I wanted to ask you about. I just heard from the plant manager before we left that the walk-down of containment showed that, I think, he said, the B line for the … pressure equalizer of the … main feed pump of the E-C-A-S—I think that's the acronym—was locked out. He's going to fill me in further when I return, but I've got to tell you, I have no idea what he's talking about. Can you give me the layman's version of what he said?"

"I'm sure the system engineers wouldn't mind giving you a short course when you have time. But until then I can cover the basics. The ECCS—emergency core cooling system—is a plant system that only operates if the water level in the core is reduced to dangerous levels. You see, the reactor core is constantly cooled down by the primary cooling water that circulates around the fuel and through the steam generators. The water keeps the core at a constant temperature. Without the primary coolant, the core will overheat, which will cause the fuel to melt. The ECCS is a backup system in case primary coolant is lost."

"The core is …?"

"The core, or reactor core, is the uranium fuel assemblies and some structural parts to keep the fuel in place. It's located in the reactor vessel. It is the source of the energy that ultimately makes electrical power. In a gas turbine power plant, the energy source is natural gas, and of course coal is the energy source for some power plants. These two types of plant produce steam that turns a turbine that generates electricity just like a nuclear plant does it. Many components outside the primary system at a nuke plant are the same as those used in these other types of power plant. The upside to nuclear fuel is that it is compact—one core can produce energy for a year or longer—versus needing a constant supply of coal or gas delivered on a daily basis. But, bottom line, it's about heat transfer: using energy from the fuel to convert water into steam to turn the turbine." Lindy found it was helpful to give the big picture so people could focus on the purpose of each plant system. McMillan continued to take notes, and so Lindy continued.

"Back to the purpose of the ECCS. The primary coolant is constantly recirculating to maintain a temperature of about 500 degrees in the reactor vessel near the fuel. High pressure is also maintained during operation. As long as these conditions remain stable, the amount of steam and electricity produced will remain constant. But if for some reason there is a break or leak in that primary coolant, the water will drain out; and if water volume decreases to the point that the fuel is not covered with circulating cooling water, the fuel will melt. To prevent this from happening, the ECCS will automatically power up when there is any indication of a leak and start pumping water into the primary system to maintain the water volume and pressure. There are four safety tanks filled with water that are ready and waiting to be pumped into the reactor core vessel if needed. The water also contains high levels of boron," Lindy paused.

"Am I going too fast?" she said, leaning forward and smiling.

"No, no, go right ahead," McMillan said. He didn't look up.

"Okay, the boron in the water absorbs neutrons, which also helps to stop the generation of heat, to cool down the reactor core. More water is available in storage tanks located in the tank yard that can also be pumped into the coolant system if needed. There are also sump recirculation pumps that return any water that has collected in the building. This entire backup system to prevent fuel damage has never been needed at West Isles. The ECCS has only been operated when required for periodic testing. It is a system that went through extensive upgrades after the lessons learned from the accident at Three Mile Island. You know, TMI lost its coolant water, which caused significant fuel damage."

"Um, okay," McMillan said, finally looking up from his notes. "I am following you so far, I think—backup water is needed for cooling during emergencies. So the ECCS didn't work at Three Mile Island?"

"The Nuclear Regulatory Commission decided that the ECCS could have performed better, so they required that additional features be retrofitted on all nuclear plants in operation after the accident. It was actually a combination of human error and lack of accurate instrument readings that caused the accident at Three Mile Island, so training requirements for operators were also beefed up along with the ECCS improvements."

"Interesting," said McMillan. "Sounds like a lot of review was done on the accident."

"You got that right. What was interesting about the accident was that if the control room operators had just left the plant systems alone, the systems would have corrected the problem. Instead, the operators thought they needed to manually adjust the water volume in the reactor vessel, so they subsequently overrode the system to adjust the water levels. But if those operators made that same error today, our updated ECCS at West Isles would override the mistake. There were many other safety features added after the lessons learned from TMI, but the ECCS changes were probably the most important fixes. There hasn't been an accident like TMI since."

"I see," said McMillan. The waiter arrived with their food, and Lindy took to eating. She hadn't eaten much that day, and the spicy enchiladas she had ordered were hitting the spot. McMillan didn't seem to mind the break either and was taking big bites of his chimichanga.

After several minutes, McMillan asked, in between bites, "Do I understand that based on what I heard from the plant manager, Cahill, this ECCS system was inoperable because of some valve being out of alignment?"

"Well, I believe what you heard was that a valve was aligned so that the pressure equalizer for one of the four main feed pumps of the ECCS would not operate. The feed pumps inject water into the primary coolant system. The valve was set so that the equalizer was locked out or off-line for one pump. If that pump went into operation, it would run for a while, and then when internal pressure built up because the equalizer was off-line, the pump would quit operating. This wouldn't be a problem, because only two pumps are needed and two are backups. Core cooling wouldn't be affected. The concern that the plant manager has is that those equalizers are always on-line, so it looks like someone purposely changed it. It had to have been changed toward the very end of the outage. The valve alignment would have been checked prior to start-up."

McMillan understood that this meant it was possible that malicious intent was involved. But it seemed like it had a minor effect, since it wouldn't have limited the plant's ability to operate safely.

"When you get back, I'm sure the engineers will go over all this again with you. Did he say if anything else was messed with in containment?"

"No, he said that was the only anomaly."

"Well, that's good news. Maybe it was just an oversight by the operators who did the walk-down, but it's still fishy. There would be no reason to lock out that valve. Maybe because of some maintenance work during the outage? There should be some records if that's the case."

"Hopefully, they will have that information when I get back." McMillan flipped through the pages to the front of his notepad. "Uh, would you have any ideas on how to sort out the people who entered containment to narrow down the field? We still have about 1,500 potential suspects."

"Let's see, there are the security records of who carded into what area and when."

"Got security working on that …"

"I heard there are a few techs working on all the radiation work permits, pulling all that were issued since the outage." Lindy's eyes suddenly lit up. An idea struck her. "You know, looking at the dosimetry records might be helpful. There might be some way to sort by radiation exposures for beta, gamma, and neutron exposures. It could give an idea of who was actually in certain sections of the controlled areas."

"Can you check that out for me?"

"Sure."

"Good. I'll let Cahill know you are working on that. Oh, is that okay? Didn't mean to overstep my authority ..."

"No, no, that's okay. Just make sure you tell Cahill to tell my boss, Al Jensen, so he doesn't chew me out for not getting my other work done."

"Will do. I'd better get back. Got plant systems training to go through ..."

"And you think you will be using that cot tonight? I don't think so."

Chapter 11

UBIQUITOUS. A NICE WORD THAT rolls off the tongue like a sentence in itself. Ever-present. Omnipresent. Allover. Universal. Most people would be shocked to discover that radiation is ubiquitous on planet Earth. Everywhere, you say? Never! But indeed, particles that are emitting radiation are present everywhere: in the food we eat, the air we breathe, the places where we live and work, and even in our bodies. Again, most people would think this was a death sentence, but in fact, nuclear radiation is what keeps Earth a thriving, life-giving planet and not a dead planet unable to sustain life, like Mars, for instance. Earth is a habitable planet because of those naturally occurring radioactive atoms. The heat from Earth's core drives the climate that we all enjoy and that keeps us alive. Without the heat generated by the radioactivity, the core would go cold, and Earth would eventually be like other planets: cold, dead, lifeless, and uninhabitable.

And if this worries you, just wait, there is more bad news about natural radiation sources. The planet is constantly being bombarded by radiation coming from the sun and deep space. Streams of high-energy particles are entering our atmosphere and exposing every living thing on the planet to radiation. With this constant exposure to deadly radiation, how is it possible that the human race even exists? How could any living thing survive? And based on most science fiction movies, shouldn't we all be some sort of mutant or superhero by now? We may not have super powers, but there is some evidence to suggest that our exposure to radiation may contribute to evolution in a good way. It may be that radiation caused some of the DNA changes in our species that created traits that improved our successful survival.

The reality is that every person on the planet receives a fairly significant radiation dose from natural sources. The antinuclear environmental activists have argued that this constant exposure to radiation explains why so many people die of cancer, but the truth of this is impossible to prove. If we had a group of people who had never been exposed to radiation their entire lives, and if they never got cancer, we would know that the activists' theory was true. But this group does not exist. To create a controlled environment that would completely isolate a group of people from all radiation sources would not be easy to accomplish. Removing the radioactive sources from the air, water, and food could be done easily enough for the control group, but preventing the bombardment from cosmic radiation is nearly impossible. Sure, you might locate the control group below the ocean, where the sheer volume of seawater would shield them from the high-energy particles from the cosmos, but who would volunteer for that. And then there are still the radioactive particles present in the human body. Removing the radioactive potassium and other elements that exist in the body would take some not so pleasant procedures. Given these challenges, one shouldn't expect this study to be tackled any time soon.

Milo understood all this. He understood that nuclear ionizing radiation was natural and that the human species had learned to adapt, if not use, the radiological effects on the body. But one thing that the body had not learned to adapt to was electromagnetic radiation. The increased sources of electromagnetic radiation were new to the planet and recently created by man. And human cells were not accustomed to the subtle effects of electromagnetic fields, making adverse, unexpected results more probable. And Milo knew that if the world didn't come to understand the danger of electromagnetic radiation, the human race would soon be extinct. A few would need to be sacrificed, but in the end it would be worth it to save the human race.

Milo saw Mietner standing at the fence overlooking the lake where they usually met. He pulled his car up and got out.

Milo slammed the door on his car, hoping to get a reaction of apprehension from Mietner. "So why'd you call? Milo told you he would call you when he had a plan," said Milo when he arrived at the fence. He was irritated that he had to leave his house to talk with

Mietner when there was no new information to share. Mietner seemed relaxed and in control as usual, which further irritated Milo.

Mietner said, "People are getting anxious. They just want to make sure that the plan is still a go. Also, they wanted an update on what you know."

Milo felt better hearing that people needed him, and this calmed him somewhat. "Milo is still working on a plan, but things are still nonroutine at West Isles. He will need more time to get things in order."

"But time is running out. Will you have something for me in the next week?"

"Maybe. Milo is working on it."

"As soon as you have a plan, you will give me a call?"

"Milo always calls. His message is important."

"Good. Good. Your message is important, but it also needs to be timely. The sooner the better for you and me. Okay? By the way, any other news about the death? How is the investigation going? The FBI is being very quiet on the status of their investigation."

"They are quiet because they have not found out who the dead guy is yet. Nothing to report. All plant systems are at normal conditions, though one valve was found to be misaligned. As I told you, Milo is not a screwup. The one valve alignment will not be traced to Milo, although Milo was the cause. The information on the valve is not something that would be shared with the public."

"Ah, that explains the lack of news. No news is good news, then. And what else?"

"Nothing else of interest to you. But Milo has been free to continue with our work. He has been making preparations, but no set plan yet to create the disaster you need. Exactly how to accomplish it, he does not know yet, but it will come," said Milo. Then he looked both ways before pulling out from under his jacket a large stack of paper, which he quickly handed to Mietner. "This is a very important document for you. Milo has redrafted his message, and you now have a copy."

Mietner glanced at the title on the first page: "The End to Civilization as We Know It."

"Of course, Milo, a very important document indeed. Getting your message out is of the utmost priority. I'm sure the staff at People for a

Safe World will agree," said Mietner, in a sincere voice. Milo was glad to see that Mietner recognized the significance of his manifesto.

"Good. Then we are fine for now. Milo hopes they will get this out as soon as possible. He will call you soon to see how that is going."

"Yes, I will be anxiously awaiting your call. This time, just to be safe, why don't you go north to town this time? Don't want to have a set pattern to our meetings that people notice. Just to change it up a bit?"

"No, that is not an option for Milo. Power lines cross the road going north. Milo will head south as usual. He's been careful, and no one is watching. Such a paranoid person, you are, Mr. Mietner." With that Milo stepped back to his car and headed toward the south entrance of the parking lot.

*   *   *   *

Mietner entered the small office in the back of Rackerby for Governor headquarters.

"We're getting there, Mr. Montague."

"Well, speed it up. It's moving too slow," Montague said with a scowl. Greg Montague sat straight in his chair, impeccably dressed as usual, his handkerchief and tie matching. He wore heavy black-rimmed glasses that made him look older than his age and deemphasized his baby face features.

"He'll come through," Mietner assured him. Mietner found Milo Parker to be very annoying and his habit of referring to himself in the third person particularly unnerving, but what could he say? You are really crazy, and I'm out of here? Not an option if he was to carry through with the plan. The people he had to deal with in this job would kill him eventually, but at least the pay was usually good. And if Rackerby got into office, his future was bright, and this motivated him. Montague had hinted that a position in the state environmental protection office was a possibility for him.

"When Rackerby gets elected and he shuts down that damn plant, you know what to do with that screwball, right?'

"Right, I know what to do."

Montague pushed back in his chair. "Good man. You'll do well on my team."

Montague reached into his desk drawer and pulled out a wad of cash. He handed it to Mietner. Mietner nodded and walked out the door.

Mietner decided to use this money to pay for supplies at the office of People for a Safe World. He would get some donuts and coffee and bring it in tomorrow for the volunteers while they made their political calls to the public about Proposition R. The calls were to remind people that voting yes on Proposition R would ensure a safe and happy future for their children. And a yes vote for Proposition R would help Rackerby get more votes. The goal was to make a telephone call to everyone on the voter registrar's list prior to election day. Ten thousand calls had been made so far, which was maybe a quarter of the registered voters. Maybe if he provided some free lunches too, the student volunteers would have their friends come down and help make the calls.

Good, he thought to himself after completing a quick count of the bills. There's enough here to feed the crew for a couple of weeks.

Chapter 12

THE FOLLOWING MORNING, LINDY STOPPED by the dosimetry office before heading to the auxiliary building to meet with Al Jensen. She was still trying to shake off the remnant of a dream she'd had that night. It was a dream about spiders: spiders in her bed, repulsive black spiders that were about to crawl on her. She had woken up in terror, trying to wipe the imaginary spiders away. She hadn't had a dream like this in a long while, and she wasn't sure why this particular dream would stick with her the way it did. Lindy was not particularly afraid of spiders, so the whole dream made no sense to her. She filed away the task to do some research on dreams when she had some time off and could get to the library.

Dottie and Jane were already working, and they filled Lindy in on the latest. Operations staff had not found any other abnormal conditions in containment. All the valves that were supposed to be in open position were open, and all the valves that should be in closed position were closed. The one valve associated with the emergency core cooling system previously found in a closed position was the only anomalous valve line-up in containment. A review of maintenance records indicated that work had been done in the vicinity of the misaligned valve, but if this was the cause of the misalignment, it was undeterminable. Jane had heard that the detailed review of security records did not show any discrepancies in those entering and leaving containment during the outage. Everyone who went into containment had a record of leaving containment. The security records had not been very helpful to the investigation, except for who had entered containment and when. The review of the radiation work permits had not revealed any discrepancies either. Everyone who had signed the safety review prior to the job had actually entered containment as planned. A review against when workers left also did not present any anomalies. Security staff, with the help of maintenance and radiation protection, were now in the process of evaluating the expected duration of the jobs in containment and comparing those numbers against when workers left containment. If someone appeared to have extended their stay beyond the time needed, they were marked down for another interview with the FBI. This was a tedious way to find the culprit and probably a long shot.

Dottie heard that the FBI was still baffled by the case. No new leads had turned up, and they had not yet identified the victim. Operations staff were in the process of walking down systems in the radwaste and auxiliary buildings, as was done for systems in the containment building, but nothing suspicious had turned up as of yet. System walk-downs were routine. Before starting a walk-down for a particular system, one of the operations staff, usually a control room operator, would get a copy of the valve line-up procedure from the document control center, which would show the valve numbers, locations, and expected positions for the mode of operation the plant was in. A written procedure for each system was necessary because the multitude of systems and associated valves throughout the plant did not allow one to do it from memory. To do a walk-down, the control room operator would physically go to each location in the facility where the system valves were located and make sure the valve was on or off as required by the procedure. Each valve was labeled with a metal tag and valve number. Some valves were actuated by switches in the control room, but others required manual operation by an operator. Aside from these walk-downs, operations and security staff were out of ideas on how to assist further in the investigation. There were no other discoveries of any malicious acts, aside for the one valve being locked out.

West Isles workers were beginning to believe that this situation of the unidentified corpse in containment might be resolved without having an unfortunate impact on the election. There did not appear to be any wrongdoing on the part of plant personnel; all had been interviewed, and thus far no one had been hauled away in cuffs. To some, stranger things than death had happened at the plant, and therefore they found it likely that the motive for the killing was probably a personal issue and not spite against the utility. It took a certain type of person to work at a nuclear power plant; and to many, that personality type included those who were willing to live on the edge and those who were willing to risk a marriage for a fleeting relationship. Such types were not uncommon and came with the risk-taking environment of a nuclear power plant.

Lindy was in the auxiliary building hallway looking at some radiation work permits when McMillan came around the corner.

"Lindy, how are you? How's your research going on the—what did you call them—atomic exposure records?"

McMillan had a smile on his face and purposely seemed to want her to complain about his greenness when it came to nukespeak. Lindy smiled back, waving her finger in admonition.

"Pulling my leg, I see. I haven't started that review yet. You know, we had over five hundred radiation work permits for the outage. It's going to take some time," said Lindy. "We had the TLDs processed as a high priority, so those reports from the outage should be in soon. Rest assured, you will be the first to be called if anything odd turns up."

"Great. Everything else has been a dead end, so I'm counting on you to save my ass on this investigation."

"Your ass is in good hands. Ask anyone, they will verify that!" replied Lindy, enjoying the innuendo. Lindy guessed it was rare that an FBI agent would dally on the job, although there should be nothing wrong with that.

"Good," said McMillan, his eyes looking keenly at her, but then he turned off the look and returned to the intense work-mode face.

"As you probably heard, we haven't gotten any leads here at the plant, either from the workers or from the condition of the facility. I'm heading off to Florida—heard that a bulk of the contractors headed over to an outage there after the outage here at West Isles. We hope to interview several."

"So, no leads on the identity of the dead guy?"

"No one at the plant had any good guesses about who it was and why this body was found where it was. Forensics said he was about forty years old and five foot nine inches tall. There was an old break on his tib—, fib—, ... his shin. Cause of death appears to be a blow to the head."

"That's not good news. A blow to the head doesn't sound like an accident, but I guess the whole situation from the beginning never really pointed to an accident."

"Yeah, pressure is building to put an end to this investigation, especially since it appears that the West Isles plant was not the target. However, the NRC will not let the plant even consider powering up until the reason for the death is determined. Hey, can you give me a call right away if your research turns up anything? Here's a number you can reach me at; it's my mobile phone."

"A mobile phone? You must rate," said Lindy, "Not too many people have one of those."

"And just in case, here's my pager. I'm serious, anything the least bit odd, you give me a call."

"Will do, Mr. FBI Man." McMillan smiled and walked away. Lindy realized she felt sorry to see him leave. She quickly brushed those thoughts from her mind and got back to work.

As she walked down the hall by the control point exit, Lindy heard the alarms from the radiation portal monitors going off. She thought it was odd that alarms would sound in both portals at the same time and decided to see what the cause was. Between the entrance and exit doors of the control point was a counter where computer stations for the radiation protection computer system could be accessed. There were two monitors located on the countertop near the entrance door, and two located near the exit door. Wooden boxes on the counters contained what looked like small flashlights. They were the same length as a pencil but much thicker. These were self-reading dosimeters and came with a clip so they could be placed on the lanyard with the security badge. These dosimeters were used to track the incremental exposure to the worker during each visit in the controlled area. It was "self-reading" because the user could look through the eyepiece at one end of the device and see the scale markings and tick marker. As the exposure to radiation increased, the tick marker moved up the scale. This dosimeter could be observed at any time, thus allowing workers to regulate their exposure. For the more potentially high exposure jobs, there would be a radiation protection escort to help monitor the situation on an ongoing basis. Workers would enter the control point room, pick up one of the self-reading dosimeters, and log onto the terminal using their name and work permit number. After their work was completed and they had gotten through the control point, each worker would be checked for contamination by stepping into one of the two portal monitors located just outside the control point room in an area not far from the step-off pads for containment entries. Once they cleared the portal monitor, the worker would log into the exit terminal and enter their dosimeter reading before leaving the control point.

When Lindy entered the room, she saw two radiation protection technicians inspecting the portal monitors with friskers. No workers were being scanned at the moment, although the alarms had stopped before Lindy had arrived.

"What's going on? Doing a calibration?" Lindy asked Jack Huston, one of the technicians.

"No. No calibration. We don't know what happened. They both just started alarming and then stopped. We were over here frisking out some wrenches and tools, and they just went off. Weird. No elevated readings that I can see. How about you, Opie? Find anything?" asked Jack.

"No, nothing," said Daryl.

"Seems pretty unusual to me. Maybe time for a recalibration by the manufacturer?"

"No, they were just checked last week."

"Is it a radon problem?" asked Lindy. Occasionally there were atmospheric weather inversions in which a layer of hot air was trapped beneath a layer of colder air. Under normal weather conditions, naturally occurring radon in the environment would dissipate, but with an inversion condition, the radon would collect and concentrate in the hot trapped air. Since the air-conditioning units pulled air from the lower layer into the buildings at West Isles for air circulation, the friskers and other air monitors located around the plant would sound alarms on inversion days because of the increased radon levels. The alarm levels on the monitors would then have to be raised to prevent them from constantly going off. Air samples would also be collected and analyzed by the chemistry department to be sure it was radon and not radioactive xenon or cesium that was causing the alarm. The monitors were not be able to distinguish which radionuclide was emitting the gamma rays that triggered the alarm, therefore, the more sensitive equipment maintained in the chemistry laboratory was needed to analyze the air samples.

"No, it's not an inversion day. We checked that earlier when the hallway frisker alarmed. It's been an unusual morning with all these spurious alarms."

"Maybe someone is contaminated and causing the alarms?"

"Checked that also. No one leaving the can caused the alarms," Jack said. However, Lindy noted there were several staff going in and out of the control point room, and many people walked past the frisker in the hallway since the hallway provided access to both the radwaste and fuel storage buildings.

"Interesting," said Lindy, not coming up with any other ideas at the moment for the cause of the spurious alarms. This was going to bother her until she figured out the cause. There had to be a reason for the alarms.

"I think I'm going to have to report this to Jensen. I know he's busy but ...," said Jack, shaking his head, not knowing what else to do.

"Before you do that, let me do some investigating. Can I borrow a micro R meter?" Jack reached under the counter and then placed a meter on the counter. After checking the calibration date to make sure it was current, Lindy took the meter and headed out to the frisker down the hall. The micro R meter was very sensitive and could measure small increases in the general area radiation and increases that the frisker might miss. Each instrument had its special use. For instance, the micro R meter is horrible at picking up small quantities of surface contamination, so the frisker is the preferred instrument in looking for contamination on the skin.

Lindy turned the volume of the micro R just high enough to hear the ticks and walked down the hallway toward the radwaste building. She did not see any deflection on the meter or hear an increase in ticks, so she headed back, turned the corner, and slowly walked down the hallway leading to the engineering building. When she reached the nurses' station, she noted a slight increase in the tick rate. She stopped and stepped back to check for the location of the highest reading. She registered the highest reading, a couple of micro R per hour above ambient, right at the nurse's door. When she opened the door, the tick rate increased. McMillan had already packed up his things since the interviews were completed, and the nurse was back at her desk working. She looked up, very surprised to see Lindy with the meter. There was also a janitor in the room, who had just emptied the trash into his large trash container and was now sweeping the room. Lindy turned off the speaker volume, knowing that it had a tendency to make non-radiation workers nervous. She also had to move up to a higher scale because on the lowest scale the reading was off the gauge.

"Can I help you?" asked the nurse. Lindy read her name badge. Gilda. She was a young, plump woman wearing bright yellow scrubs and white athletic shoes. She looked annoyed that Lindy had entered her domain.

"Just doing a survey, don't mind me," said Lindy, as she continued to walk toward the janitor and his trash can. Raul Jimenez was used to people with meters, so he didn't bother to stop his sweeping and paid little attention to Lindy.

Lindy was eyeing the trash can, and sure enough, there was a relatively high reading near the trash can. Aha! Someone had disposed of radwaste inappropriately in regular trash! She pulled the trash can closer, expecting the reading to increase, but it did not. Curious. Then Lindy walked closer to Jimenez, and the reading began increasing again. The high readings were coming from Jimenez!

Raul Jimenez had worked for the West Isles plant for ten years and had to have been in his fifties when he first started. His job was to do a sweep of the restrooms and offices during the day shift and try to get a head start on the trash collection for the night shift. If he had time, he would clean handrails and occasionally mop up a spill, as long as it was not in the controlled area. The closest he got to the controlled area was to empty the trash cans kept under the counters at the control point. The work was easy and fit his needs, since in his later years he was not capable of doing much more. Lindy had always liked Raul and his non-contentious attitude and enjoyed chatting with him.

"Raul, can you help me for a second? I've got something that I need help in moving," said Lindy.

"Sure, Ms. Andrews," he said, resting his broom on the trash can. Raul's face was splotched on one side as if burned. Lindy had heard he had been in a car accident many years earlier.

"Down at the RP office, come with me," Lindy said, as they headed back to the office just two doors down from the control point. "How you been doing?"

"Muy bueno, Ms. Andrews, but maybe better if I was younger."

"Have you had any medical exams lately?" Lindy asked. They were now in the radiation protection office where Cal Sherwood, the radiation protection supervisor, was working at the desk.

"Well, yes, I have. Yesterday I was at the doctor. My doctor, he check my heart, but it is good. No problemo," Raul said with a grin.

Lindy showed Cal the meter reading, which immediately got his attention. He looked at Lindy, knowingly.

"Was the test your doctor did, was it a heart stress test?"

"I think so, Ms. Andrews. You know the test? I passed the test," Raul said, very proud of himself.

"Did the doctor tell you the exam would involve radiation?"

"I think so. He said many words. I think he said X-ray?" Lindy was not surprised to hear this. The doctor probably gave a very long and detailed discussion of the heart stress test to Raul and may also have explained the test's radiation dose in terms of the dose received from a chest X-ray. The heart test involved the injection of a radioactive isotope of thallium, which had a short half-life and would be gone in a few days. The radioactive thallium would collect in the heart and was used to show how well blood flowed through the heart. The radiation dose to a patient receiving this procedure would be small and well worth the risk in relation to the knowledge gained by the doctor. Most patients did not expect to be "hot" after the exam was over, even though it would have been explained. And most patients would never know they were more radioactive than normal, since most did not own a radiation meter.

Lindy was considering how to break the news to Raul that he was causing alarms to go off around the plant. Although the dose was small for Raul, the radiation levels given off were easily picked up and would be for a couple of days until the material in his system decayed.

"Raul, the doctor gave you a little radiation so he could run the very important heart test. It was important for the doctor to know how well your heart is working, and it was a good thing that he did the test. But ... our instruments can still pick up a little of radiation from the procedure. Do you understand?"

"But the test is over? And I passed?" Raul looked a little concerned.

"Yes, you passed. Your heart is muy good. But our instruments are very, very sensitive, and the test you had is interfering with them."

"Que?" said Raul, still looking unsure.

Cal jumped in to help out. "Raul, you are fine, but it is our instruments that have a problem, so we are going to have to give you a few days off. Is that okay? We need you to be away from our instruments, and it would be best if you stayed home for a couple of days."

"Vacation time?"

"You won't need to use your vacation. It is free vacation for you. Would you do that favor for us? It would really help with our instruments. They can tell you had a test, so we will need you to stay home for a couple of days until the instruments are working better. I will have Al Jensen talk to your boss right away. Okay?"

"Es okay. Should I go home now?" Raul was looking much more cheerful, now that he heard the instruments were having the problem.

"Yes, let me walk down with you to Mr. Jensen's office, and we will make the call to your boss," said Cal. Turning to Lindy, he asked, "How many days do you think he will need?"

"At least three, but to be sure, have him return next Monday. And recheck him."

"Okay, Raul, let's go. We will need you to be away from work until Monday. Could you do me a big favor and check with me when you return. We will want to make sure the test material is gone."

Lindy was glad Cal was in. When it came to explaining radiation, Lindy found it impossible not to think in technical terms. Cal was good at figuring out the bottom line of concern for people and could skip the technical mumbo jumbo. It was something she needed to work on.

Chapter 13

LINDY ENTERED THE INSTRUMENT CALIBRATION lab and found Maisie busy working on a radiation meter.

"Maisie, what are you doing here?" said Lindy, surprised to see her working with instruments.

"Wherever I'm needed, that's my motto!" Maisie responded, almost cheerfully, but with underlying sarcasm. Normally she would be doing radiation surveys or providing the safety escort for containment entries. A radiation protection technician was required for any person or group that enters the containment building to take radiation measurements and also to check for removable contamination prior to any maintenance. "Norm is out sick, so they asked me to help out."

Norm Callaway was an institution at the plant. He had started as a document/records technician back when the plant first went online in 1974. Norm had found that repairing instruments was something that suited him. It was a low-pressure job and required a meticulous person to keep the records. Half of every day was spent on maintaining records for the inspectors from the various controlling agencies. There was nothing more worthy of a monetary fine from the NRC than performing a survey with an out-of-calibration instrument. Each meter was labeled with the calibration date and due date, usually three or six months later. Frequently the meters needed no adjustments, but if that due date had passed and you did a survey using it, the data was useless as far as the inspectors were concerned. The requirement made sense because of the radiation exposure accidents that had occurred in the past due to some lazy technician who didn't bother to check his meter.

"Low woman on the totem pole, I see," Lindy said.

"Hey, what happened to sister solidarity. Don't be badmouthing me! Besides, I'm working hard! Look at these Model Threes!" Maisie pointed to a couple of instruments that actually had dents on the bodies. "It's like the gorilla from the suitcase ad had a shot at them. Some are in pretty bad shape."

"Now you are comparing technicians to gorillas. You are really looking for trouble!"

"True, true. I like to live dangerously," said Maisie.

Lindy saw a neutron instrument on the table that had several dents and some large scratches on the meter box and appeared beyond repair.

"What's with this meter? Geez, did the person who was using it live through the trauma? This is major damage."

"I don't know about that one. Norm hadn't put it in the log to be repaired or serviced out. And everyone thinks he keeps good records— it's news to me," Maisie said, shaking her head.

"He will have to service it out with that damage. You know, I could use it for my radiation safety training—a lesson on how not to treat your meter. I'm sure Norm won't mind if I take it," said Lindy.

"So how are things going?" asked Maisie. "Okay coming home to an empty house?"

"Yeah, it's fine. This whole dead guy thing has kept me preoccupied," said Lindy as she walked to the back of the room where Norm's desk was located. Norm liked electronics and was known to have the latest software and computer equipment for his use. He had a new computer and a monitor that looked sleek and modern. On the screen was something Lindy had never seen before. There was a picture of a Coke can, and it was in color and slowly rotating. Lindy couldn't get over how real it looked. Prior to this, she had only seen monitors that had a black background with white or green letters. This looked like a television screen.

"Maisie, did you check out Norm's computer? It's got a color picture of a Coke can, and it's moving—that is cool!"

"Yeah, I thought so too. Norm told me it's something new; it's called a screen saver. He says it will prevent screens from getting ruined in the future," said Maisie. "Did I hear right that a certain FBI agent has also been keeping you busy?"

"What? Where'd you hear that? There's nothing going on between McMillan and me. Doesn't everybody have better things to do than track what's happening in Lindy's life?" Lindy said.

"Why are you surprised? Come on. Dinner at Mamacitas? You knew someone would notice," Maisie replied, somewhat heatedly.

"Yeah, I guess you're right. This McMillan guy wanted to meet some place where the press wouldn't be. I don't know about that guy, though." Lindy scrunched up her nose. "I'm not sure if he's my cup of tea. He's just so ... so corporate. Did you hear if Sievers noticed?" She hadn't seen or talked to Sievers in days. She had tried to call him but kept getting his voicemail. She wondered if they would ever be friends, much less lovers, again. She wondered if she even *wanted* to be friends with him.

"No, no word on what Sievers thinks, but lots of talk about you and ... what'd you say his name was? McMillan?"

Lindy had underestimated how quickly gossip could travel. She was only slightly disappointed to hear that Sievers had not heard about her dinner and found that odd. At one point, she thought the world had ended when Sievers said he was moving out.

"Yes, McMillan, Sawyer McMillan. Well, if a dinner conversation gets people talking, so be it. Nothing is going on."

"Just between you and me?" Maisie could read her better than anyone.

"Okay, just between you and me. He seems to be an okay guy. He's pretty serious about his job, though, and doesn't seem to be looking for a relationship."

"But?" Maisie could sense something more in Lindy's voice.

"Okay, I think he kind of likes me. I can make him smile on occasion. And he gave me his mobile phone number."

"He wants you to call him?! That sounds pretty serious."

Lindy could sense the excitement in Maisie's voice. Maisie thought her husband, Andre, was a real catch. She kept hoping that Lindy would find a good mate like the one she'd found.

"Well, he gave it to me so I could call him right away if I have a clue for him or any information that would help the investigation."

"A clue? I'm sorry, Lulu, but that just doesn't count. Sounds like he's using you for your mind only. He needs your help is all."

Lindy felt some disappointment at the response and could tell Maisie was trying to let her down gently by using her pet nickname for her. Maisie had seen Lindy's struggles with men and how Lindy always went for the unattainable, only to find herself disappointed in the end.

"But isn't that better than having the guy drooling over your body? I mean, needing me for my mind, that's a good thing, right?" said Lindy, hoping for some positive feedback.

"Listen, if he ain't drooling now, he will never be drooling for you. You gotta have that instant chemistry, that sublime reaction, or else it will never work."

"That's harsh, Maisie. Are you sure? Is there no hope for friends becoming lovers?"

"Nope," said Maisie. Maisie thought she had missed her calling to be a marriage counselor but made up for it by practicing on her friends.

"Oh, well, maybe Sievers heard about my 'dinner date' and is jealous. It would be good to get some mileage out of it," said Lindy, who was again looking over that neutron meter, still impressed with the damage. "Anyway, I had come by to see Callaway. But since he is out and you probably know nothing about his filing system, I will let you get back to work and look for him tomorrow."

"Okay, Lulu, but give me a heads up on your next dinner date so I can at least rebuff some of the bullshit when I hear it. I can't be takin' care of you if you don't give me some warning. You hear me, girl?"

"I hear ya, I hear ya," said Lindy as she walked out the door.

Lindy's next stop was the document and design control office. The staff of this office was responsible for ensuring that any procedures used in the plant were the most current and accurate. The staff also controlled all the diagrams associated with plant systems and structures, so that whenever a design change was made, the diagram could be updated. These were critical functions for all nuclear power plants. If the design of a system changed the valve configuration, it was important to update procedures so that the operations staff knew the correct valve position under the new design. Another set of documents maintained by DDC office was the vendor records for the nuclear-grade parts and supplies used throughout the facility. If a part was found to be defective, even at another nuclear plant, a notice would be issued; and, if necessary, wherever that part was used at West Isles, it could be located and replaced. It took a good-sized staff to maintain all these records, and the manager tended to hire good-looking young women, which is probably why Lindy found Thumper loitering at the counter, chatting up one of the young women. Lindy also noticed that the room seemed to be particularly chilly, and she grabbed her upper arms to warm herself.

A different young woman came up to the counter. "Can I help you?"

"Yes, could I get a working copy of procedure number RP dash DOS dash 59? Thanks," said Lindy, and the woman went to the rows of files to find the original current version of that procedure to make a copy.

Thumper didn't pay much attention to Lindy, which was fine with her. Looking around, Lindy noticed that several of the young women wore sweaters, and she wondered why they kept it so cold in this office. There was another thing that several of the women had in common: their nipples were prominently showing through their tops. Now the temperature of the room was starting to make sense to Lindy.

When the young woman returned with the copy of the procedure, Lindy asked her, "It seems awful chilly in here. Is it always this cold?"

"Oh, yes, it has to be. The boss said that the area needs to stay cool for the copiers and other equipment we have here," the young woman said innocently.

"I see," said Lindy and left the office. Lindy was surprised to see that Thumper was the only man hanging around, considering the protruding situation. She guessed there was no harm done and, on the good side, at least some young women had the jobs instead of the typical white male. She would talk with the women one of these days about their boss, but there was no time for that today.

Chapter 14

AT THE END OF THE day, Lindy was at her desk in the dosimetry office. It was six o'clock in the evening. The door opened and in came Wade from the training department. Wade was about thirty-five years old and stocky. He wasn't bad looking, with his marine hair cut, wire glasses, and space between his teeth, but all together he looked like he dropped out of the 50s and even looked like a black-and-white movie character. Despite that, Lindy had always liked Wade. He wasn't into the head games that other guys liked to play. He seemed a lot more comfortable around women, and conversations seemed to flow easily. Too bad he was married.

"Look who the cat dragged in. Haven't seen you in awhile, Wade, not since they moved the training rooms to the other side of the plant. How is it in the back forty?" Lindy asked.

"Same as the front forty, I imagine." Wade sat on the edge of Lindy's desk and thumbed through some of the papers she had on her desk. "Just been doing a lot of quick training classes to odds and ends types, you know, such as coroner assistants and FBI investigators. I even had some guys in one class who wouldn't say who they were with." Wade quit looking at things on her desk and grinned at Lindy.

"Hey, would you have time to do my whole body count now? I'm going to be out of spec in a couple of days—even with the extension."

"For you, I guess I could warm up the counter. It's going to take a few minutes before it's ready—have time?" said Lindy. She got up from her chair and headed to the door to go with Wade to the whole body counter trailer.

"Sure," said Wade as he followed her outside.

The sun had just set behind the rolling hills, but there was still a slight glow to the sky. The crisp cool air from the delta was rolling in, and the birds were nestling in for the night, barely making a sound. But for those damned flying spider webs, this was Lindy's favorite time of day. Several strands were crossing the wooden stairway leading to the white trailer, and she had to break through them to reach the door.

Lindy unlocked the trailer, which had the vendor's name written in large blue letters on the side. Whole body count systems were expensive, so West Isles leased a unit from Mergeson. It was pretty much a necessity, since everyone who entered the controlled area had to have a whole body count. A whole body counter measured the amount of radioactive material that was deposited in a person's body, usually in the lungs or digestive tract. The whole body counts also showed the normal background concentration of naturally occurring radioactive potassium in the body. The measurements were performed and stored mainly as a protection against lawsuits. Sometimes someone would come from another facility with a large amount of radioactive material in their body that they had inhaled or ingested. Some types of radioactive material would eventually be flushed from the body; but others were more persistent and could remain in the body for years. Lindy had never seen it, but there had been a few workers from one of the Department of Energy weapons facilities who had body burdens from plutonium inhalation. They could not talk of their work at the weapons facility, but there were sometimes hints of occasional accidents during the manufacture of the plutonium pits that are used in nuclear weapons. The health consequences were often negligible from these intakes of plutonium, but even so, the Mergeson counting system was very sensitive and could detect their presence. Relatively speaking, the radiation level of the body's radioactive potassium was much higher than any dose received from small amounts of inhaled plutonium. From a scientific point of view, the potassium was much more harmful but naturally present, so it could be ignored by the dosimetry program.

"Do you mind doing the coffin? It doesn't take as long to warm up," said Lindy. She pointed to a unit on the floor that was a box the size of a coffin surrounded by four-inch walls and a metal unit that rolled on tracks on top of the walls over the entire length of the box. Many people, both men and women, could not handle lying in the coffin, even though the overhead unit was only about a foot wide, leaving plenty of open space as it traversed the body. For this reason, there was a stand-up scan unit located at the other end of the trailer. It looked like a tanning bed, only upright. There were slots for the hands to slip into; the person would stand with their back facing out. Most people did not have any problem with a whole body scan in this stand-up unit.

"No problem," said Wade. "Have you heard yet who the dead guy was?"

"No. I heard the FBI still doesn't have it figured out." Lindy sat at the control panel and typed in Wade's name and badge number while the counter warmed up. "The FBI agent did comment, though, on how weird we nuclear workers are. I gotta say, it's sometimes hard to defend us."

"That's no joke. I really wonder how some guys pass the MMPI. I mean, isn't that test supposed to weed out the crazy ones? I don't think the psychiatrists have it figured out as well as they pretend. I was doing a systems class the other day, and there was this one guy who said men should be allowed to have several wives."

"A polygamist? Was he from Utah?" Lindy said. Lindy had heard that there were areas in Utah where polygamy was still practiced.

"Not sure," Wade said, shoving his hands into his pants pockets. "Oh, and then there was a guy who kept asking me about the cooling systems and going on and on about how bad electromagnetic fields were for people. I think his name is Milo. How's that for a weird name? He said that cells in his body could sense the EMF doing damage to them—kind of like ESP, only it was his cells talking to him. I reminded him that Earth has an electromagnetic field around it, but he said that wasn't harmful because it wasn't strong enough. He did think, however, that ionizing radiation was good for you and was trying to convince the other people in the class to go for the dose. Now, how does someone like that get past the system?" Wade said, shaking his head.

The Minnesota Multiphasic Personality Inventory, known as MMPI, is a personality test developed by the University of Minnesota to provide information on a person's personality strengths and weaknesses. The nuclear power plants were required to ensure that workers were stable and well-adjusted and capable of being successful on the job. The test provided the employer with an outside opinion about job applicants and whether they would do well in the nuclear power plant environment.

The test included over seven hundred questions that required true or false answers, and it appeared to Lindy that the same question was asked several times, although worded differently each time. It took about three hours to answer the questions. She thought it must have been designed to wear down one's ability to lie consistently.

"I don't know, Wade. All I know is that MMPI nailed me. I was so irritated about answering all those stupid questions, over and over again; it was, like, how many times did they need to ask me if I liked flower arranging? And then the questions about having diarrhea and dressing in women's clothes were just ridiculous. Of course I like dressing in women's clothes! It was such a discriminatory test against women that by the end I was just giving any answer just to tweak the test reviewer."

"That must be part of the test—how long you can persevere. Why would anyone need a seven-hundred-question test?"

"That's true, but then I had my interview with the psychiatrist about my results, and he mentions that I have a rebellious tendency and asked me if I knew what brought that on. Now, how could he figure that out from all those crazy questions? There were no questions on being defensive or rebellious …"

"Yeah, I know what you mean. The sex questions really got to me—seemed to be awfully personal and unrelated to working at the plant, so I lied about most of those. The psychologist said I suffered from sexual hang-ups …"

"Did he suggest help for those hang-ups?" Lindy liked flirting with Wade since he took it lightly and rarely thought it was serious.

"Yeah, he said I know this woman who is very rebellious that I should look up." Lindy laughed with Wade.

Wade continued in between laughs, "Now, I want to know how someone like Thumper passed that test. You gotta guess that he lied through his teeth on those questions, or else he'd be wearing an ankle bracelet right now. His mind is always in the gutter. But then, who knows? Maybe answering honestly gets you a gold star."

"Thumper getting a gold star—now I've heard everything. Hey, the coffin's ready. Let's get this count done." Wade laid down face up in the box. Once he was comfortable, Lindy started the count, which caused the overhead detector to begin moving down its track.

While she waited for the scanner to finish, Lindy thought about that interview with the psychiatrist. He had also hinted that her rebellious nature had something to do with her relationship with her father, but she had no clue what it could be. Of course, she had problems with men, but it wasn't because of anything her dad did or didn't do. She was just gullible and needed to quit believing everything she heard. She regularly dismissed what the psychiatrist said, but the question always seemed to come back to her. Her dad was a good guy, a little screwed up, but a good guy. He's the one that got her interested in science by reading *Scientific American*. What could be wrong with that?

Chapter 15

DOUG DEAVERS SAT AT HIS computer terminal, staring at the screen, not sure what to write. The editor in chief of the *Valley Sun* had liked his articles and printed his stories covering the investigation of the finding a dead body at West Isles, but now there was a void of information. Doug called the public information office at the utility and also the FBI, and both said they had no updates for the public. It was the usual story: the investigation continues, and if anything new comes up, we will inform the public, blah, blah, blah.

Many papers across the country had carried the second story Doug wrote about the West Isles incident, although not the *New York Times*. Doug had interviewed a local resident, Jarvis Hamel, who said that he had symptoms of radiation poisoning. Hamel said that he distinctly remembered that his tongue was itchy on the day the dead body was found. In his experience, his tongue only itched when the nuclear power plant was releasing radioactive gases. Doug found the statement to be a bit incredulous but decided to put it in his story anyway. He told the city editor, Sam Bozworth, that Hamel didn't seem quite with it, but Bozworth liked the story and printed it as is. The other stories that Doug wrote for the *Valley Sun* were more down-to-earth but did not have legs and were not carried by any other papers, much to Doug's disappointment.

The paper had posted a reporter and cameraman at the entrance of West Isles. So far they had not been able to interview anyone with new information. Most of the workers would not stop and talk with any of the reporters, and the environmental advocates didn't have any information beyond their usual rant. Doug had called his contact at the local sheriff's office, but he too did not have any information. Doug was desperate for something new to report. He tried to think outside the box on who might have information. He randomly flipped through his Rolodex, hoping for insight, when the Rolodex stopped with the business card of People for a Safe World. Doug had used information provided in their press releases for his stories, but he had yet to call the office. Maybe they had current information.

Doug dialed the telephone and waited for a response. "Hello? Can I help you?"

"Is this the office of People for a Safe World?"

"Yes, it is. Can I help you?"

"I would like to speak with Art Bigsbee. Is he in?"

"Yes, let me transfer you."

"Art here. What do you want?" said a male voice at the other end of the line.

"Yes, this is Doug Deavers, with the *Valley Sun*. Do you have time for a few questions?"

"Why yes, I do," said Bigsbee, now sounding more cordial.

"I was calling about West Isles. I have your press releases, and it appears you have some serious concerns about the facility."

"Of course we do. Anything that is a danger to the environment and people is of concern to us. Are you the one that's been writing the news reports for the paper? It appears that you are somewhat aware of the lies that are being perpetrated by the utility, although I believe you downplay the harm the facility is causing. You should be more straightforward with the public." His voice sounded high pitched, and his accent screamed Maine. Doug imagined him with shoulder-length hair, a tie-dye shirt, and stone-washed jeans.

"Well, we try to provide all sides to the story, I hope you understand. The current situation with the dead body is very interesting. The authorities are not providing any more information about the mysterious death or whether there were malicious activities at the facility. Would you have any information that we've not covered?" Doug knew he was going out on a limb in expecting this organization to know anything about the status of the investigation, but he figured there was no harm in asking. If the recognized authorities were not willing to share information, he was forced to look to other sources.

Art, on the other hand, was considering whether to share with this reporter the latest information he had received from his source. Tom Mietner had never said the name of the person that he was in contact with who worked at the plant. Art found it best if he didn't know. But he did know that the investigations at the plant had turned up something that had yet to be reported by any news outlet. Art was sure the information was true, although explaining how he knew was not an option. The question now was whether sharing the information would provide more value to his organization and whether the contact would continue to be a source of information in the future. Losing the source would be devastating to their activities. However, the authorities were clearly withholding facts, and people had a right to know that they were being lied to. With these issues in mind, he decided that sharing would bring more value to the organization, but he would be very careful not to provide any identifying facts about the source beyond the fact that the person worked at the plant. That obviously couldn't be avoided.

"It's interesting that you should ask that question at this time. We recently received some new information. We were just working on a press release. We may have it out later today." Art was unusually calm now.

Doug could see that he was being led by a carrot, but he did not care. If the information had any merit at all …

"I tell you what. Let me hear what you have, and we can discuss the newsworthiness of the information. What do you say?"

"Well, I guess it's probably my duty to tell someone about this, but it doesn't look good for the utility. We heard the identity of the corpse is still unknown; however, the more significant news is that during inspections of the facility, several safety systems were found to have been compromised. Our information is that the entire safety system designed to ensure the integrity of the dangerous reactor core and fuel was compromised, and that none of the plant operators noticed. Those people are idiots. "Idiots!" Art shouted. "They have no idea what they're doing. It's disgusting how they are putting all our lives in danger. My source says that this could have allowed the melting of the radioactive fuel, which could have resulted in the China syndrome. The China syndrome! It is clearly a sign that the facility cannot operate safely and that a major accident could happen at any time and threaten the lives of those who live near the facility."

"China syndrome? What is that again?" Doug knew the term—who wouldn't after the movie—but wasn't sure how this syndrome related to what had happened at West Isles.

"The China syndrome? It's when the fuel melts and is no longer in a safe configuration. What you get is a mass of uranium ore that continues to create a radiation discharge because the chain reaction is out of control. There would be no way to stop it, and it would churn and boil forever, possibly sinking deeper and deeper into the Earth, spewing out radiation continuously, making the area for miles around uninhabitable for thousands of years. There would be nothing that we could do to stop it. Of course, the uranium mass wouldn't really reach China, but you get the idea."

"This is serious," said Doug, thinking that at the tour of the power plant on media day, this wasn't discussed. How could the government allow the nuclear plants to operate if something this dangerous could happen, even if it was only remotely possible? The consequences would be irreversible. Doug would have to do more research on this syndrome, but he was thinking that a bubble blurb next to one of his West Isles stories that discussed the China syndrome would be very interesting to their readers.

"No shit, Sherlock. We will be mobilizing organizations across the country to put an end to the use of these dangerous nuclear plants." Art appeared to be in his stride, truly animated by his mission.

"Can you tell me where you heard this information about the safety systems so I can do my cross-checking?"

"Really, now, you know I cannot share a name. But off the record, we have an inside source, someone who is involved in the inner workings of the plant. Under no circumstances would we compromise this source."

"Yes, but how reliable is the information? And this compromise of safety systems—was it on purpose? Is there some unknown organization working to cause a catastrophic accident at the plant?" Although Doug was worried about public safety, the reporter in him was also interested in the scoop. Maybe this would get his byline in the *New York Times*.

"Our source says the systems were compromised on purpose. Who did it we do not know. As you can see, causing a serious accident at the plant is not impossible. Anyone with a basic knowledge of the plant can cause a catastrophic accident. People for a Safe World strongly opposes nuclear power for this reason. It is not safe, as demonstrated by the current situation at West Isles."

Doug debated with himself about how to proceed with this information. Clearly, People for a Safe World had an agenda, but this information was compelling and clearly information the public should be aware of. Doug would need to obtain some verification from the utility or the FBI on what was found, but how to get that information? Could he fly just with what this organization said? Hopefully, Bozworth would find that acceptable, or maybe some well-crafted questions to the company's public relations department could confirm some of the information.

"Do you know what safety systems were affected?" asked Doug, wanting to make sure he had all the facts.

"No, just the system that protects the fuel from melting. I'm sure the utility can fill you in on plant systems that protect the deadly uranium fuel."

"Did your source have any guesses on what happened to the dead guy? I mean, how could a person just go missing at the plant and nobody notice?"

"That's our concern also. The utility keeps touting what a great security staff they have, and then this happens! No information on the dead guy, but we think the death is somehow related to the safety system, which is something West Isles would not want to discuss in public."

"Okay, well, thanks for the information. Do you mind if I quote you?"

"Not at all, feel free. And keep up the good work! We need all the help we can get to protect people from the scourge of nuclear power. It must be eliminated for the good of mankind."

Doug hung up the phone but then picked it up again and dialed the number of the pubic relations department that he had now memorized from dialing it so frequently.

"West Isles Power Plant. Margaret Colliers speaking."

"Ms. Colliers, glad I reached you. This is Doug Deavers, from the *Valley Sun*. I'm working on another article on West Isles for tomorrow's paper. Would you have any news to report?"

"Let's see. Plant personnel continue to support the investigation into the cause of the death, but nothing new to report on that front. You might try the FBI. They don't always get back to us on their findings. Otherwise, some maintenance work is in progress while the plant is shut down and systems can be accessed."

"I will try the FBI, thank you. Ah, one thing I did hear is that West Isles had a close call and barely averted a meltdown of fuel, that one of the fuel safety systems was not functioning correctly ..."

"Wait one minute. No such thing occurred. Who told you this?"

"A source who prefers to remain anonymous. But you did have a fuel system problem occur, isn't that true?"

Doug could sense that Margaret was hesitating on the other end of the telephone. This indicated to Doug that there was some truth to the information, but how much was fact and how much fiction, he did not know.

"I'm sorry, Mr. Deavers, I do not have any information that would indicate a major failure in a safety system. If you had more details, I could check it out with plant personnel?"

Doug looked at his notes to make sure he used the right words. "There was a failure in the emergency core cooling system is what I understand."

"Okay. I can follow up on that and get back to you. Is tomorrow okay?"

"Well, I need to have my piece ready for the boss's review by five this afternoon. I think the boss will be okay with going with the unconfirmed story that it was possible that a major accident was barely averted at the power plant and that we are awaiting details that should be forthcoming from regulators and West Isles. We would like to have an official statement from West Isles, but we could run without it if necessary."

"I understand. I will return your call as soon as possible. Good-bye," said Margaret and hung up the telephone receiver. Doug knew he would get a callback soon.

*   *   *   *

"Tom, it's Art Bigsbee," said Art into the telephone receiver, fidgeting in his chair. Tom Mietner had been a major help to his organization, and besides having the contact at West Isles, he also provided quite a bit of resources and money to help the cause. Tom had recruited students from the local college to make calls to the voters to remind them to vote yes on Proposition R. He had also arranged the purchase of signs and actually had crews who posted them around town. And his involvement with the Rackerby for Governor organization could be useful in the future. Art thought that some of the money that Mietner provided may have originated from the campaign, but he was careful not to ask. For all these reasons, it was important that he stayed in Mietner's good graces. "I just got a call from the *Valley Sun*."

Art listened for a minute, then said, "Well, I thought it best to tell him about our concerns with the safety systems at West Isles. ... No, no, I didn't mention your name. I'm sure it was obvious that we have a source who works at the plant."

Again, Art listened while rubbing his forehead. "Uh-huh, I understand all that, but we have a serious situation at West Isles that needs to be addressed! Believe me, this will only help our cause. Unless the public learns how the utility is covering up its problems, they will never be stopped. I'm sorry you don't agree with how I handled this, but I think it's for the best." Art hung up the telephone, kicked back in his chair, and sighed. He couldn't please everybody.

Chapter 16

THIS COULD GET INTERESTING, THOUGHT Margaret Colliers as she considered how to best handle the situation. Kramer Chomsky, the public relations director and her boss, would ask if she thought the newspaper would run the accident story regardless or if it was just the reporter's way of getting a quick response. Based on the previous articles that ran in the paper, she had no doubt that the reporter was serious. Margaret was finding that every day it was getting harder to maintain a positive image of West Isles and could only look forward to the day when the vote would be over. However, the finish line seemed further away with each passing hour, and she prayed that no further disastrous events would occur. This newspaper story could signal a turn for the worse if West Isles did not come clean on what was discovered.

Five years ago, Margaret Colliers, slender, blonde, and what could best be described as perky, began working in the public relations department at West Isles. When she graduated from college with a degree in journalism, she went directly to the local newspaper for a job. Her first assignments involved covering local community events, writing obituaries, and fixing the local police logs for print. But her real desire was to be a serious investigative reporter, and as with all fresh reporters directly out of school, she hoped to make a difference in the world with her writing and reporting. In the evenings, she would write short stories and articles on women's issues for magazines. She got one story on a struggling writer published in *Woman's Day*, but the article did not get her much notice, and therefore she turned to working on the newspaper's editor to allow her to pursue more serious pieces. He agreed to allow her try her hand at serious reporting as long as her other work was not compromised.

When looking for story leads, she stumbled across a local issue of kickbacks and possible bribes that appeared to involve city politicians. During a casual conversation with a friend, Margaret heard of some interesting coincidences involving a local developer and how he had miraculously convinced the city council that a new strip mall was needed where a local park was currently located. Local residents protested fiercely to protect the park but to no avail. The council voted for the strip mall, citing the city's desperate need for the increased tax revenue that would be generated. Sensing that there was more to the story, Margaret decided to do some research and looked into the public tax records of the council members and the developer and found that he had made substantial campaign contributions to some council members. Additionally, some members reported that they had received gifts and speaking engagement honorariums from a company that had very close ties to the developer. Margaret could not believe that the connection was so obvious and thought she would have a guaranteed headline story to take to her editor. But before she did that, Margaret needed to get a statement from the developer and therefore arranged for an interview. The interview seemed to go well even though no confession was made and the developer emphatically denied having received a quid pro quo for his donations. When she returned to her office, however, her editor informed her that she was barking up the wrong tree, that there was no story of interest to the public, and that she should move on. Because she had some substantial documentation to the contrary, this confused her. But her editor insisted that the public was not interested, and he also hinted that it was not acceptable to disagree with him. She got her first rude awakening to the real world of newspaper publishing some months later when she found out that her editor was friends with the developer. There were many more such lessons, and eventually the drudgery of the work made her decide it was time to move on.

During this time, Margaret married her long-time boyfriend, Ted Colliers, whom she had dated in college. He was a mechanical engineer and had a job at a local engineering firm. When Margaret said she needed a change, it was clear that this would require them to move from the area. They decided that Ted's employment options were more limited, and so his résumé was circulated first. The most appealing job offer came from the nuclear engineering department at the West Isles Nuclear Power Plant, much to Margaret's dismay. The salary was good and there appeared to be lots of opportunities in other departments in case this job didn't pan out. Ted tried to assure her that he would be safe and promised not to go into any radiation fields while on the job. Margaret had heard that radiation could make a man sterile and didn't want anything to go wrong since they hoped to start a family soon. After much discussion, they decided this looked like a good opportunity.

After moving to Brownsville, Margaret interviewed with the editor at the *Valley Sun*, but she sensed many similarities between her previous editor and the *Valley Sun* editor and found the idea of doing the same thing she had done at her other job both discouraging and dreary. Ted had heard about a job in the community relations department at West Isles and suggested she interview for the job. The dangers of radiation scared her. Although Margaret also felt strongly about the menace of nuclear power, she decided to interview. The pay and the short commute made the job very appealing, so she decided to put her fears aside and try the job out for size.

And now, five years later, she found herself not only working for the utility but actually enjoying the daily challenges of defending the facility while trying to educate people on the safety of nuclear power. Her fears and concerns about the safety of nuclear power had dissipated, and she now believed that nuclear power was safe due to the rigorous backup programs and inherent safety designs at the plants. She was responsible for writing press releases that explained the intricacies of plant operation and safety protocols in simple terms that almost anyone could understand; in the process, she had learned a surprising amount about the operation of a nuclear plant. Her knowledge came in handy when listening to Ted talk about his day at work.

After speaking with this reporter, Doug Deavers, and listening to his questions, Margaret sensed that the facility might be at a crossroads that could change the future of West Isles. Margaret knew that a misaligned valve had been found and that it could have had some impact on safety of the reactor core, but so far this information had not been made public. The FBI had asked that the information be withheld, because they believed that releasing this information could compromise their investigation. Margaret, however, knew that withholding the information could have a devastating effect on the credibility of West Isles and the utility. She had expressed this concern to her manager, the director of community relations, but he vetoed her recommendation that they go against the advice of the FBI. That decision now put them in a bind. The worst thing that could happen right now was to let this reporter go forward with his story about a narrowly averted meltdown and not challenge it. Recovering credibility after such a story would be impossible, especially since a safety system had been compromised, even if only minimally.

Margaret lightly knocked on the director's door and heard a muffled "Come in" from inside the office. She entered and saw her boss hunched at his computer screen. Stacks of printouts, binders, and file folders were piled on every surface and in every corner of the tiny office. His bookcase was crammed full, not with books but with Houston Astros souvenirs. Newspapers and reference material were strewn across the floor. She wondered how the man found anything in such chaos.

"Sorry to bother you, but I just had an interesting call just now, from Doug Deavers, you know, the reporter from the *Valley Sun*. He is threatening to run with a story tomorrow that we barely averted a meltdown. He heard that there was a failure of the ECCS. I think we need to put this to rest right away by clarifying the findings."

Kramer stopped tapping on his keyboard and glared at her. "How did he find out about the ECCS?"

"An anonymous source, but it has to have been someone who works here. Nobody else would know."

"Any hope of stopping the story?"

"I don't believe so. He's gone with marginal information in past articles. The editor has given him lots of leeway."

"Okay, let's call Cahill and have him inform the FBI that we need to nip the situation in the bud."

Chapter 17

LINDY WAS BACK AT HER desk in the dosimetry trailer the next afternoon with a stack of paperwork in front of her. Some of the reports were from people who had worked during the outage. She had promised McMillan that she would look through the reports and see if there were any unusual results that could help in the investigation of why the unknown man was murdered and his body left to rot in containment. The review of security records had not turned up anything unusual. Clearly someone had made sure that the victim's security badge was put in the card reader to show that the victim had exited. There had to be some sleight of hand, for the suspect would also have to have inserted his own badge in the card reader. Then, when the shift ended, the suspect would have placed both badges with dosimetry in the security drop at the exit gate before exiting the controlled area. That would be easy, since no one would be watching closely at the security drop. Anyone working at the plant would know that if they wanted get away with leaving someone behind undetected, they would have to card out for the person. Some *Mission Impossible* scenario was not needed to figure out how the suspect got away with the deception. Given that the only unusual condition found in containment was one misaligned valve, the murder was probably not related to doing any damage to the plant. A simple murder was all, nothing to get all alarmed about.

The local papers and environmental activists, however, were trying to squeeze whatever mileage they could get out of the continuing unknown cause for the death. Every day, the *Valley Sun* had an article about the status of the investigation of the mysterious death of an unidentified victim. Since there hadn't been much official information, the paper had resorted to interviewing anyone who could provide salacious details about the investigation. After the NRC stated that there were no radioactive releases or safety concerns, a reporter interviewed nearby residents who had information that a substantial release of noxious radioactive air had in fact been released from the plant. One local resident, Jarvis Hamel, said that he noticed immediately that his tongue became itchy, a symptom of radiation poisoning. The public information officers from the utility could explain that radiation may cause cancer but not itchy tongues, and they were at a loss as to how to deflect such nonsense. How could anyone take the story seriously? Of course, the story left out the fact that Hamel had delusions and thought the government was sending X-ray beams to his house on a regular basis, or that he lined his clothes with aluminum foil and always wore an aluminum hat to protect himself from the X-rays that were sent to harm him. Jarvis also thought that it could be the telephone company, Ma Bell, that was targeting him. Yet an itchy tongue sure seemed plausible to most readers since, who knows, look what happened to the Spiderman?

After several reliable sources confirmed that no release had occurred, the *Valley Sun* turned to insinuating unhealthy and extreme aspects of the mysterious death. Experts came out of the woodwork to be interviewed on what they believed to be the reason for the death. Reports of gruesome disfigurement were circulated, indicating that extended radiation exposure had created a monster. It was lucky for everyone the person was dead, they reported, for if the person were alive, he might have become a modern-day Frankenstein. It was certainly a good reason to shut down the plant immediately.

On other days, the newspaper reproduced old articles claiming to show how cheap natural gas was by comparison and questioning why the company bothered with nuclear power when there were safe alternatives.

Although some of the articles gave the plant workers a good chuckle, the public relations battle was beginning to wear on everyone. Many felt strongly that nuclear power was the way of the future and that to be independent from oil, the nation needed to embrace other options. There were downsides, of course, but every energy source has its problems. Fossil fuels pollute the air; wind power kills birds and can't supply power when the winds aren't blowing. Hydroelectric power plants kill fish; geothermal plants create noxious brine wastes containing lead, arsenic, and zinc; and solar needs batteries to work effectively, creating heavy metal waste problems for future generations. No energy source comes without a cost. But oil and coal are still the cheapest and therefore the most prevalent. Nuclear plant workers had evaluated the downside of nuclear power production and found it to be no more hazardous than any other method and believed that their work was an asset to the public. So the pay wasn't the only thing that motivated them to invest their time in the job, because there were certainly easier ways to make money. What was really confusing was that other countries had realized the potential of nuclear power and had gained independence by generating their own power and recycling their energy dollars by reprocessing waste fuel. Rather than give a percentage of their national gross product dollars to another country, they kept their wealth. Keeping American dollars in America seemed like such a basic principle for future security. Even the laborers and mechanics who scraped by in high school and had no special training or background in economics understood its importance. Why didn't the general public understand this? Additionally, nuclear power is much more efficient than other energy sources. But instead of looking at all this, the United States continued to send dollars to foreign countries in exchange for oil. Nuclear power plant workers tended to think like blue-collar workers. They were proud of their country and wanted to ensure success for future generations, and they believed that nuclear power was a necessity for a bright future. It was interesting that environmental activists who thought nuclear power would eventually destroy the planet were also concerned about future generations. There was such a chasm between the two types of people that many plant workers would not tell their neighbors where they worked. And no one wanted their kids ostracized at school because of where their father or mother worked.

Lindy took a deep breath and sighed, looked at her watch, and noted that it was just about quitting time. Maybe she would take a break before hitting the reports. She left her office and stepped into the main dosimetry office area where Dottie and Jane were busy at the computer terminals.

"Hey, boss," said Jane.

"Hey, Jane," Lindy replied, "just about time to head home."

"Yep, just finishing up this last personnel record," said Dottie, who had a family waiting for dinner. She reached for the filing cabinet where she stored her purse while still entering a few last entries, then said, "Done!" And out the door she went.

Jane was still keying in information and asked, "Hey, still no word on the dead guy? Funny thing. I thought it might be my husband, but I found him home in his Lazy Boy, so I guess we can scratch him off the list."

"Jane, you are not married."

"Oh, yeah, guess it was just wishful thinking that the dead guy was my ex." Jane was one of the few women who had to pay her ex-husband alimony. He had pleaded poverty because he couldn't keep a job due to his drinking, and since Jane made a pretty good salary, the judge awarded him a year's alimony until he got on his feet. The year was just about up, so things were looking up for Jane.

"I hoped it was your husband too, then at least the mystery and anxiety would be gone and we could get back to the business of making watts. Although I would have visited you in jail after you were caught for the murder. Nobody else would spend the energy to knock off that ex of yours."

"You are so right. By the way, I hear you have a direct line to the FBI. What have you heard?"

"What direct line? Just because I went to dinner with McMillan?" said Lindy. Jane nodded and winked. "God, can everybody just get over it! He needed some information about radiation and plant operations. In any event, he didn't know much about the murder before he left to interview contractors."

"Jeez, Lulu, you could have pumped him for information for your most loyal workers. We do have a reputation to maintain," Jane said with a straight face.

Lindy laughed and asked, "Do you know anything?"

"Not too much on the grapevine about the dead guy. Fingerprints didn't turn up anything, and there are no missing person reports matching the description. Heard security didn't find anything unusual, and the walk-down of the aux and radwaste buildings didn't turn up anything. Although," Jane paused and then lowered her voice, "I did hear that Mike Dire got real nervous when he was interviewed by the FBI."

Lindy arched an eyebrow. She wondered why the operations manager would be nervous.

"A review of the rad work permits didn't show any unusual activity," Jane continued in her bubbly manner. "As a result, I think your FBI friend probably has a fire lit under his butt right about now to come up with something."

It was amazing the information that Jane and Dottie had. They were better informed than Al Jensen, the radiation protection manager. Jane and Dottie had missed their calling as interrogators; anybody walking in the door would unwittingly divulge all their knowledge without even realizing it. And they guessed right that McMillan was feeling the pressure.

Lindy asked, "What's the general consensus among the managers?"

"Word is that it's looking good to be your basic murder due to one of the seven deadly sins. Me, personally, I'm rooting for envy, my favorite deadly sin, but such a silly, reckless sin. Why be envious when you can get revenge?"

"Seriously, I guess that's a good thing," said Lindy.

"I think the managers think so. If it's something mundane, then we'll be able to go back online. With the election coming up, we need to have some days at power, making bucks for the investors and keeping people's houses cool without running up the costs," said Jane as she gathered her purse and sweater.

"I tell you, the *Valley Sun* hasn't been too helpful with its reporting." Lindy shrugged to show her disappointment.

"Yeah, you should have seen ole Jarvis Hamel strutting at the local market, as if he was some big celebrity, looking ridiculous as ever in his aluminum suit. Susie at the market said that Jarvis buys about five rolls a week of Reynolds. He's got to have some stash of aluminum at his house—not that he would let anyone in to see. If people reading the paper only knew ... well, I'm going to head home. Don't work too late."

"Have a good night." Lindy walked to the door with Jane. And as she left, Norm Callaway appeared at the steps.

"Norm, what are doing out here?" asked Lindy. He seemed to be in a hurry.

"I heard you took my neutron meter. I came to get it back," he said hastily.

"Ah, Norm, I was hoping you wouldn't be needing it since it's in such bad shape."

"Sorry, but I need it back right now."

"Okay. Just hold on. I have it in my office. But you can't repair it—it's a wreck."

Lindy came back a few moments later with the destroyed meter and said, "I wanted to use it in the training class I do once in a while on radiation safety. I can use it show people what's inside these babies."

"I need it back." Norm spoke with a serious tone as he took the meter out of Lindy's hands. "I need it for spare parts." He quickly left the trailer.

Now that was strange, thought Lindy. Norm seemed rather tense. He was always a bit wound up, but he seemed more wound up than normal. The uncertainty at the plant must be getting to him. Lindy locked the trailer door—things just hadn't seemed the same since the body was discovered. Until they found out the reason for the killing, everybody was being a little more conscientious about safety.

Lindy headed back to the stack of reports that were waiting for her and intercepted the ringing telephone on her desk.

"Jensen here. Andrews, I need you to report to the community relations office right away. They need you to talk to a reporter."

"What? Me? Why me? I've never spoken to a reporter before!"

"I know, but they specifically asked for someone like you. They need a certain result, you might say, and are looking to put a soft face on the typical power plant worker. And they also need someone who knows health physics. Sorry, but I couldn't think of anyone else."

"But ..."

"You'll be fine. I gotta go. Now get over there now, and I'll talk with you later about how it went."

Lindy hung up the phone and found her hands shaking slightly. A softer face? What does that mean? Does the deer in the headlights look qualify as a softer look? That was all she thought she had in her at this moment.

Chapter 18

THE SIMULATOR BUILDING WAS THE only permanent building outside the controlled area. It housed an exact copy of the West Isles control room and was built as a training facility for reactor operators. The operators could be trained to manage the power plant in all different operational modes, including accident scenarios. Every switch, gauge, button, and panel was an exact duplicate of the control panels at the plant. Software had been developed that allowed the instructors to choose a scenario and then have the panels alarm and respond as they would in the real control room. The simulator had turned into an excellent training tool, and the program had received good reports from the regulators and insurers. The accident at Three Mile Island had been caused in part by human error, and this simulator allowed for the accurate training under a variety of accident scenarios. There were classrooms in another section of the simulator building, but due to the lack of available office space, they had been converted for use by the community relations department. It turned out that this was a better use for the space, because visitors could tour the simulator and visit displays while discussing how nuclear power works; this eliminated the need for visitors to enter the controlled area. The simulator satisfied most visitors' curiosity about the power plant. The Japanese had demonstrated that visitor centers at their nuclear power plants were effective in calming the fears of the public because they helped remove the mystery and made nuclear power seem less exotic and more "normal." The West Isles visitor center had been designed with that hope, although polling information showed that it appeared to have had little effect on local public sentiment.

Lindy found Margaret Colliers sitting in her office, and together they headed to the conference room.

"I'm sorry, Lindy, that I dragged you into this. But I believe you are the best person to communicate with this reporter," said Margaret.

"I hope you're right, but I don't know how I can help here," said Lindy, as she settled into a chair at the conference table.

"In the past," said Margaret, "I've had male engineers talk with reporters about the plant, and it hasn't produced the best results for us. The men tend to be stiff and speak down to the reporters. As the interview goes along, I can see in the reporter's body language that they sense the condescension, and later it shows in the reporter's article. I was hoping to try something different this time."

"What's that?"

"Communication studies have shown that women tend to show more empathy and come across better at being reassuring and sharing the concerns of others. Also, our local paper and the reporter who's been generating a lot of articles lately, Doug Deavers, has gotten some bad information from an anonymous source, and we need to stop this story before it gets blown out of proportion. You heard about the misaligned valve?"

Lindy nodded.

"Well, someone has interpreted that to mean that West Isles almost had a meltdown of the core."

"Impossible!"

"Yes, that's true. However, it is also the crux of our problem. How do we credibly deny this without sounding like we are trying to cover up something? Why hadn't we been proactive in providing information on the minor valve misalignment when it was discovered? It is an easy leap to think that we were hiding the information. We got Cahill to agree that the best thing to do was to come clean and explain exactly what we found. It was the FBI's request to keep it quiet. Cahill will give them a call to explain our position. But this is where you come in. Inherently, being a woman makes you more credible and caring."

"I don't know how to be those things."

"Yes, you do, just by being yourself. I've attended your radiation safety class in the past, and you are what we need, so don't worry.

We've got some time before Deavers shows up, so let's go over some basics. Number one, try to stay away from acronyms—they drive reporters nuts. Two, don't talk about anything that's outside your area of expertise; if you are not sure, say so, and we can get back to him with a right answer. It's okay not to know everything. And three, relax. Think about this as if you are giving a training class and you'll be fine. I'll cover the questions about the ECCS but will be looking for you to answer any radiation safety questions."

The telephone on the table buzzed. "Mr. Deavers has arrived."

Lindy was surprised at how young Doug Deavers appeared. His writing made him seem much older. He didn't appear nervous, but he did seem to be in a rush. He sat down immediately at the table and flipped through the pages on the yellow pad he carried until he found a blank one.

"Thank you both for meeting me at this late hour. My readers will be glad that I got your side of the story."

Margaret proceeded to go over the operation of the emergency core cooling system and used system diagrams to help explain which valve had been locked out and why it would be inconsequential to the safety of the plant. "So, as you can see, even if extra cooling was needed, there were still three operable pumps that could supply cooling water."

"Why wasn't this information shared with the public when it was discovered?"

"That is a question better answered by FBI. However, I believe there was a concern that sharing the information could compromise the investigation. In any event, it now appears that this valve may have been locked out during maintenance work and missed being returned to its open position."

"And you have evidence of that maintenance work?"

"Well, no. But it's the best conclusion for the circumstances and …"

"Could be hopeful thinking, too. I would say that that kind of narrow thinking could hamper finding the killer. By the way, any information yet on who the victim was?"

"No, but the FBI is handling that end of the investigation."

"Don't you find that a little odd? It seems that uncovering the identity of someone who had to have clearances to get into your facility would not be that difficult. Maybe there is something more going on than meets the eye?"

"Mr. Deavers, now I think your imagination is starting to cloud your sensibilities. Remember that during our outages we have many people come in from around the country to assist, and it's going to take awhile to contact them. Considering the circumstances, it's going to take some time," responded Margaret. Her voice was even, but Lindy could sense that the reporter had struck a nerve. Deavers continued to write on his yellow pad, appearing unfazed by her response.

Deavers continued. "On another issue, some local residents believe that there was a release of radiation from the plant and that they had symptoms that confirmed it. Do you have a comment on that?"

Margaret looked at Lindy for an answer, and then Lindy sat forward in her chair and said, "Well, as you know, the Nuclear Regulatory Commission confirmed our conclusion that a radiation leak did not occur. So there should be no symptoms, but aside from that, the symptoms reported ..."

"You mean like the report of an itchy tongue?"

"Yes, such as that report. There is no scientific evidence to confirm that such a symptom would occur. Sir, can I ask you a question? Have you had X-ray pictures taken of your teeth when you visited the dentist?"

"Yes, I have."

"The amount of radiation that your tongue received when those pictures were taken was pretty substantial. Did your tongue itch?"

"No, not that I recall. I don't remember feeling anything."

"Exactly. The radiation from a dental X-ray machine is no different than radiation from nuclear power. If there was a release of radiation, it would not be detected by sight, sound, touch, or taste."

"We also had reports about the body that was found, that radiation affected its appearance. Is that true?"

Lindy looked at Margaret to see if she was going to answer that question. Deavers looked at both of them, waiting.

"The coroner's report should provide you with detailed information on that issue. However, Lindy, do you have anything to add, since you were there when the body was discovered?"

Lindy nodded and said, "The injury to the person had a much greater effect on the body than the amount of radiation the body was exposed to. The radiation the body received while in containment would have certainly caused some significant health concerns, if that is what you are asking. On a microscopic level, human cells can be damaged by radiation, but the visual effect would appear similar to any other bodily harm from any other carcinogen. There would not be a dramatic change in the body."

"You were the one that discovered the body? Inside containment?"

"Yes, along with a reactor operator."

"Doesn't that worry you? I mean, working around radiation? Aren't you concerned about your health?"

Lindy had answered this question many times before in casual conversations. It was interesting to her that people had such a skewed view of risks in life. Being in a moving vehicle carried one of the highest risks for fatality, but people willingly get into cars every day without worry.

"You might find this surprising, but I do not worry at all. Since I am always monitored, I know what my radiation exposure is. And I know that the potential for health problems for me in the future are very low given the radiation dose I receive. Mr. Deavers, living on this planet does not come without risk."

Doug Deavers asked a few more questions and then quickly exited to meet his deadline.

"Okay, that went well, I thought," Margaret said, heaving a sigh of relief.

"Yeah, real well," Lindy said. In her mind, she replayed what she had told the reporter. "But we won't know until tomorrow's paper, will we?"

Chapter 19

GREG MONTAGUE AND TOM MIETNER stood in the back of the Elks Club. It was a good crowd, about fifty, not a bad turnout for a weeknight. They listened as Rackerby finished up his speech: "... and there are better and cleaner options than nuclear power that would not put the public at such a risk. When you elect me governor, one of my highest priorities will be to support alternative energy sources. It is a lack of support on government's part that has prevented successful alternatives. I am not beholden to big oil, so I can follow through with this commitment."

There was a smattering of applause, the most he'd gotten during the speech on any subject. Considering the older age of most of the attendees, Montague thought this was a good sign. This more conservative audience appeared to agree that nuclear power was not the best option. He smiled at Mietner. The election was only a couple of weeks away, and it was still too close to say whether Rackerby or Conrad would win. Tonight Montague hoped to hear from Mietner that he was making good progress with his contact at West Isles. With Conrad taking such a strong stance for nuclear power, it made sense that if something were to happen to West Isles, it would hurt Conrad and catapult Rackerby into the governor's office.

Montague nodded to Mietner, and they both headed out into the refreshing air of the evening hours in suburbia. They found a location away from the door, and Montague lit a cigarette.

"Rackerby is going to win this. You can bet on it," said Montague.

As Rackerby's campaign manager, it was mandatory that he say such things.

"Yes, he sounded good tonight—confident, sharp, on the ball," said Mietner, looking sincere.

"How are things going on your end? Time is getting short, you know." Montague eyed Mietner closely. He wondered whether this guy had it in him to do what's necessary to get Rackerby elected. He hoped so. A lot was riding on Mietner's success. Montague knew from experience that at this point the election could go either way, but he wanted a sure thing.

Well, there's going to be an article in tomorrow's paper that should be interesting and good for Rackerby." Mietner hesitated for a minute, appearing unsure of himself. "I expect it will discuss how the utility has been involved in a cover-up … and that the safety systems at the plant were compromised, which could have allowed a meltdown."

"A meltdown? That's serious. And that's good," said Montague, smiling.

"Yes, my contact said that it was of concern to the FBI as well, but the public has not been made aware of it. The People for a Safe World believe that the death is probably associated with the plant problem and also that it shows how vulnerable nuclear power plants are to disaster," continued Mietner.

"Yes, I can see that. It certainly validates Rackerby's contention that nuclear power is too dangerous. This could be good."

Mietner was grinning now. "I think so."

"But we need to clinch this. How's your guy doing? Everything proceeding as planned?"

"Things have been tough for him since the body was found, what with all the scrutiny, but he's working on it."

"Good, but the clock is ticking, so you need to keep pushing," said Montague.

The sound of the clapping had died down, and people were now leaving the hall. Rackerby came out, surrounded by several people who continued to ask him questions. Montague crushed his cigarette on the ground under his foot and stepped over to assist Rackerby.

"Thanks, folks, for coming, now, Mr. Rackerby has to get going. He's got a busy day tomorrow," said Montague, as he hustled Rackerby into a waiting vehicle.

Chapter 20

LINDY STARED OUT THE DUSTY window in her office. The empty, unlighted parking lot was softly backlit by lights from the controlled area. She had spent about two hours going over the dosimetry records of workers who entered containment during the outage. The results she had reviewed so far were typical—mostly gamma radiation with a little beta—but some reports indicated low quantities of neutron exposure. Some low-level neutron doses would have been recorded on the dosimetry badges of those workers who had been in the vicinity of the reactor vessel. Workers were usually only allowed near the reactor when the plant was in shutdown mode. The entry at power that Lindy and Chris made was very unusual, which is why a radiation protection technician went as an escort to constantly monitor the radiation levels. When the reactor was at power, the neutron levels in certain areas would have been too high to allow anyone to stay in the area, especially if the work required more than ten minutes. But with the reactor control rods inserted between the fuel rods, the chain reaction was essentially stopped, so only an occasional stray neutron could escape from the reactor vessel. The control rods were made of boron, which acts like a sponge when it comes to neutrons, soaking them up and thus preventing them from bombarding uranium atoms in surrounding fuel rods. However, a few stray neutrons escaping from the reactor would have caused the low-level neutron doses on the badges. The gamma radiation coming from the reactor vessel and metal parts of nearby systems was a residual effect caused by the constant bombardment of neutrons while the plant was at power.

Lindy had never witnessed a neutron overexposure of a person and hoped to never experience it. Beta-gamma overdoses looked just like an extreme burn from heat and were gruesome enough on their own. Neutron overdoses were more sinister. Neutrons do not interact with the surface layers of the body but instead do their damage in underlying tissue. The skin, eyes, and hair would all look normal, but a terrible destruction would be occurring inside the body, where neutrons were gradually obliterating the internal organs, muscles, bones, arteries, and connective tissues. It was similar to a sublimation effect, where a solid is converted directly to a gas, bypassing the liquid phase. It would truly be an experience of the walking dead; the person might look normal for a few minutes, but then the bones give way and the skin falls like an empty sack on the ground. Whenever Lindy considered a neutron overexposure, it made her think of the Star Trek movie where Spock sacrificed himself to save the ship. Spock did not die immediately when he stood in the extremely high neutron field generated by the ship's power reactor. That much was accurate. But if they had wanted it to look truly realistic, they would have had a much more gruesome final shot of Spock in that reactor room.

The phone on Lindy's desk rang and made her jump—she was not expecting any calls at this late hour. She picked up the receiver and gave her rehearsed greeting, "Dosimetry, Andrews."

"Hello, Lindy, this is Sawyer McMillan. Sorry to call you so late, but then, I didn't expect you to be in. Thought I would leave a message," said McMillan.

Lindy sat up in her chair at the sound of McMillan's voice. "Uh, yes, I'm here doing some research, um, the reviews you had asked for."

"I hoped you wouldn't have to work after hours to review them."

"I would have been here anyway—I would be doing these reviews eventually." Although she had not worked late in a few months, Lindy didn't like the insinuation that she was doing this work just for him. "Do you have news?"

"I do. We believe we have found the murderer and have the suspect in custody."

"Great!" Lindy jumped out of her chair. Finally, some resolution. "And the lucky winner is?"

"The name won't be released until tomorrow, but since you've been working so hard, I guess I can break the rules. Obviously, don't share this with anyone, but we have in custody a man named Carl Osman," said McMillan.

Lindy did not recognize the name. McMillan continued. "He worked at West Isles during the outage as a laborer."

"How did you find him?"

"To make a long story short, we finally got a missing persons report of a man who fit the dead guy's description: Mr. David Worth, a transient laborer who worked at power plant outages. He was reported missing by family members. It took the family awhile to realize Worth was missing. Apparently he wasn't good at staying in touch."

"But what does that have to do with this Osman guy you mentioned?" Lindy had to jump in. Where was the connection?

"Hold your horses, and let me finish. Mrs. Amy Worth, also a transient laborer, married to one David Worth, was having an affair with Osman. During her interview, Amy was reluctant to admit it at first, but then when she saw that she would be one of the main suspects in her husband's murder, she began to open up. David Worth and Carl Osman had been friends and went drinking together after work on several occasions. Carl and Amy had started a secret affair, and it appears that David must have found out. Amy says she knew nothing about the murder and actually seemed surprised about his death. David Worth was notorious for disappearing for lengths of time—one of the reasons why Amy wanted a divorce. They had decided to go their separate ways while they were at West Isles, so she did not know that he had never left. She fingered Carl, saying she found Carl had quite a temper and in recent months things were getting serious between them. She said she wouldn't be surprised if Carl had taken a swing at her husband when they were at West Isles."

Wow, thought Lindy, it was just your basic seven deadly sin murder. She was very relieved by the news. "And has Osman confessed?"

"No, he says he's innocent—typical. He ponied up for a lawyer pretty quick. But we've got records of him in containment at the same time as Worth on at least two occasions, and we have motive. That's enough to hold him for now. And there was a report from a worker that he had seen a disagreement between Worth and Osman. We had so many reports of fights that this one didn't stand out."

"Who reported seeing them arguing?"

"I'd have to check my notes to be sure, but I think it was Mike Dire." Interesting, thought Lindy, the one who was nervous during his interview with the FBI.

But it was good news that the killer had been identified. Lindy could sense that the world was already resetting to a normal state. But then it occurred to her that McMillan might be finished with his investigation and wouldn't need to return to the plant.

"This is great news! Hopefully we will back online soon now that destroying the plant was not the ulterior motive behind the murder. And I guess that means you are done with your investigation?"

"I've got a lot of work to do still to shore up the case. I will be heading back first thing in the morning. That's why I called. I thought maybe we could go to dinner again?"

"Uh, I've taken a lot of heat for the last time we had dinner together—like it was some official date or something ..."

"I understand ..."

"Like I had some inside scoop. I couldn't walk down the hall without someone bugging me."

"I understand ..."

"But hey, what the heck. People need to eat," Lindy said, trying not to sound too excited. And dammit, Sievers still hadn't returned her phone calls.

"Good. Maybe I will see you tomorrow, but if not, I will call and let you know when would be a good time."

Lindy hung up and wondered what she was getting into. Why get involved with someone who will be long distance? Stop it, she told herself. It's just dinner. She went back to her records, although now all she could think of was what she would wear tomorrow.

Rather than start in where she left off on her work, Lindy looked through the stack of reports that were in alphabetical order, found the *O*s, and flipped past a few to find the one for Carl Osman. She found his record and glanced quickly over his dosimetry results. He had some finger ring results; nothing unusual there. An experienced transient laborer would do some of the heavy cleanup work in high radiation areas where finger rings would be used. Most utilities tried to keep the exposures low for their own staff, and therefore contractor staff would usually get the highest radiation doses during outages. Lindy noted that there was nothing unusual on his monthly badge. She pulled the report from the stack, knowing that someone would be asking for it soon. Then Lindy looked through the *W*s for Worth. There were two reports—one for Amy and one for David. Amy's report had all zeros. She must not have done much work in containment. Lindy then looked at David's report, expecting the same, but she noticed a reading for low-energy gamma. This was unusual. Most readings for gamma were high energy, because the main source of gamma exposure was from radioactive cobalt, a high-energy gamma source, and radioactive cesium, which also would show up in the high-energy chip of the dosimeter. The low-energy gamma reading could be attributed to many things, from being in an area near radwaste or possibly an error with the badge. On occasion, dosimetry badges had gone through washing machines when inadvertently taken home by workers. There was a special evaluation done for that situation. Lindy thought it best to think about this with a fresh mind, so she prepared to head home. She wanted to be fresh for tomorrow—baggy eyes from lack of sleep would not do.

Chapter 21

THAT EVENING AT THE OFFICE of People for a Safe World, Art Bigsbee surveyed the crew of students who were stationed at the bank of telephones and making calls to voters in the district. Each student had a list of voters obtained from the county registrar's office and a cross-checked list of telephone numbers obtained from a vendor company for a fee. The noise level in the room was high as the students talked on the telephones, especially whenever they got very adamant about the dangers of radiation with the voter on the other end of the line.

Bigsbee waited while one of the students finished his conversation and put down the handset.

"Alex, how's it going? Looks like the calls are moving along. Have you had a chance to check the tallies?" Each caller had a tally sheet to record whether the voter they contacted was for or against Proposition R, the proposition that would shut down West Isles.

"Hello, Mr. Bigsbee, things are going good. And I did look at the tallies earlier. Did you want to see them?" Alex rummaged through the papers on his desk and found a stack of tally sheets.

"Good, thanks," said Art, taking the paperwork. "Can you let everyone know we will have a brief meeting in about, let's say, five minutes?" Alex nodded and started passing the word around.

Bigsbee took the tally sheets with him to his office and sat down. On the top sheet Alex had written down the results from each tally sheet and had added up the columns. This wasn't a scientific analysis of voter intentions, but it had been found to be useful for detecting trends in voter sentiment. Tom Mietner was very interested in this data and had regularly asked for updates. The notes that Alex made today indicated that 156 voters indicated they would be voting yes on the proposition, 112 voters said they were voting no, and 92 voters were still unsure. Based on these results, it appeared that the proposal to shut down West Isles would be approved, but Bigsbee had found that the phone tallies were a bit skewed compared to the scientific polls done by Rackerby's campaign. The difference was probably due to people wanting to please the students while on the telephone. Clearly, the students were thrilled when they thought they had a voter who agreed with them, and who wouldn't want to make the nice-sounding boy or girl on the telephone happy? But there was a slight increase in the yes votes in today's tally as compared to the previous few days.

Bigsbee suspected that the increase was due to the recent article in the *Valley Sun* that included graphics showing what would happen if the China syndrome were to occur at West Isles nuclear plant. Actually, the article presented a hybrid version of the syndrome and didn't quite relay what Bigsbee knew the syndrome to be. He disagreed, for example, with the statement that the uranium mass would quickly cool and could be dealt with in a matter of years. His understanding was that the mass would spew and churn for thousands of years. He would have to call that reporter, Doug Deavers, and get him the scientific articles that his senior scientists had provided proving this fact. Also, the news article downplayed the damage that could have resulted from the misaligned valve in the emergency core cooling system. He was very disappointed in Deavers, although it was clear that his article was having some positive impact on the voters. The article was scary enough, it appeared, to affect some voters and remind them of that movie, *The China Syndrome*, and the accident at the Three Mile Island nuclear plant. Tom Mietner would be pleased when he saw these latest tally numbers. Art checked his watch and headed back to the students.

The students were milling about, getting coffee, and chatting in small groups. When Art walked in, they all stopped and gathered near the phone banks. Art looked at the fresh, young faces, and it reminded him of his youth. He wished that he had used his time when he was young more wisely. In the hours he wasted away smoking pot and drinking beer with his college buddies, he could have actually contributed something to society. If he had just listened once in awhile in his business finance class, maybe his finances for the organization would not be in complete disarray. At the time, however, his main concern was avoiding the draft, and staying in school was the easiest way to do that.

"Thank you all for your support of the organization, and I also want to thank Alex for being such a great recruiter in bringing you all here for this important cause. Be assured, you are making a difference in the world. Every call you make is one more way for people to understand the dangers of nuclear power. Nuclear power is not as safe as the authorities would like us to believe, which has been demonstrated of late at the West Isles plant. If you did not hear of or read the article in the *Valley Sun*, the West Isles executives deliberately covered up the fact that a major safety system was compromised. And while this safety system was compromised, it could have allowed a major accident at the plant to occur, one that would have caused large amounts of deadly radiation to escape into the environment, killing thousands of people and making the surrounding areas uninhabitable for years." Art noted that some of the kids gasped, but others looked surprised, which was good.

Art continued. "Some of you look skeptical, and I can understand that. If it is so dangerous, how can they allow nuclear power plants to continue to operate across the nation? Well, you all are probably too young to understand human hubris, but as you gain more experience with the internal workings of different people that you will meet in your lifetime, you will find that some men think they are above the laws of Nature, that they can control things that are really out of their control. That is what I think these engineers and executives that run these nuclear plants believe—that they can control those uranium atoms so that there is never an accident or problem. But Nature has its way of doing the unexpected, and it's just a matter of time before man finds out just how little control he has. There will be more accidents like Three Mile Island and probably worse accidents too. So we need to stop them now, and the best way we can do that is to use their own legal system against them. We need to get Proposition R passed and shut down West Isles!" Art slammed his fist against the table, making the kids jump. He had their full attention now, and most were nodding in agreement.

Alex said, "Right on." A few kids even clapped.

Art caught his breath for a second and then continued in a quieter voice. "And we are not stopping here. Once we finish this election and close West Isles, we will move on to the next facility, and then to the next facility. And it will be with your help that we save humanity from those who think they are smarter than Mother Earth. Now, I will let you get back to your phone calls. Don't forget to remind the voters to read that *Valley Sun* article. Thank you all for the hours you spend calling the uninformed voters." Art left the room as the students quickly sat at their seats and eagerly began dialing.

Chapter 22

MILO ROLLED INTO THE PARKING lot of the overlook as five cars revved by, clearly showing their irritation. It's the small things in life that keep you going, thought Milo. Milo went back to contemplating the news he had for Mr. Mietner. He was internally celebrating, knowing that Mietner and the others needed him. He had a solution to the problem that Mietner desperately needed solved. Also, he was looking forward to seeing what kind of loyalty Mietner really had for his cause.

Mietner was nowhere to be found in the parking lot. Milo parked in his usual spot, turned off the engine, and sat low in the seat. About fifteen minutes later, Mietner finally pulled into the parking lot. They met in front of the cars, again looking over the lake, the sun long gone and the shadows deepening.

"You're late," said Milo, not disguising his unhappiness.

"Very sorry—out of my control. Won't happen again," said Mietner.

"Better not. Milo almost left, taking his news with him."

Mietner's eyes narrowed. "I'm glad you did not leave, because the People for a Safe World need you. Everyone is counting on you. You had called?"

"Yes, Milo has a plan to get that accident that you wanted."

"Fantastic! We knew we could count on you."

"But he will need help."

"Not a problem, whatever you need. Just tell me."

"First things first. What is the schedule for release of my manifesto?

121

You've had a chance to read it, right? It's an important message that needs to get out to the world."

"Yes, of course, your manifesto," said Mietner. He rubbed his chin and tapped his forefinger on his nose. "Ah, the senior scientist is ... is looking at it tonight. Yes, tonight. And we ... we have a meeting scheduled tomorrow to discuss when and how to release the document to the world so that it has the biggest impact. Some were thinking that it would have it's biggest impact after the accident at the plant, you know, the most relevance."

"Any time would be a good time. It's a timeless message," Milo was disappointed to find his message delayed.

"Hey, look, we've got the experts looking at it, and if we release it now, I'm sorry to say, it could be ignored. Don't you want to be sure the message is heard?"

"Of course."

"It's never good to be too rushed in these things."

"I guess, maybe you are right."

"The senior scientist thinks so, and he has experience in bringing information to the public. Okay, then," Mietner continued, "you were saying you had a plan to cause an accident. That is great news. Everyone at People for a Safe World will be very happy."

"Yeah, Milo has a plan, but he will need help," said Milo.

"Sure, any help you need, whatever," said Mietner.

"Milo's plan is very good—guaranteed to produce an accident, significant enough to discredit the safety of nuclear power. Of course, Milo does this to make sure his manifesto is heard. The short-term loss will be outweighed by the fact that the world will finally truly understand the cost of the machines that generate electromagnetic fields. Nuclear power is not bad. It's the electricity it produces that is bad for humans."

"I know, I read your manifesto. So true," said Mietner.

"Here's the plan," and Milo described what was needed to make the plan work.

*   *   *   *

Mietner left the meeting with Milo not feeling well. He had been able to keep his distance from Milo up to this point, but what was needed now would bring Mietner front and center into the conspiracy. It was not going to be pleasant, but in the long run the outcome would help Rackerby get elected. Sometimes extreme measures were necessary. Rackerby's opponent, Thomas Conrad, had clearly stated that he advocated nuclear power, and Rackerby's team had determined that this was a weak point for him with the voters. Most people do not believe that nuclear power is a good idea and believe instead that other safer sources should be used. However, Conrad was gaining in the polls and shrinking the lead that Rackerby had early on because, it was thought, he was taking a strong stance against raising taxes and he advocated reducing the size of government. The lead was slight at this point, but Rackerby was not getting traction on other issues. Although Montague spoke strongly about Rackerby's future success, other political hounds did not think this was necessarily the case. Montague had promised him a job in the capital if Rackerby won, something he felt was an important step for him to gain contacts and eventually run for office himself. If Rackerby lost, Mietner would be back in Stillwater, Oklahoma, working at his father's law office, processing wills and managing divorce cases. He didn't want to go back there. No, not at all.

Chapter 23

THE NEXT MORNING, LINDY WALKED by herself to the auxiliary building. She was thinking about the dream she had that night. It was a spider dream, but with a different twist than all the others. Instead of the spiders being on her, they were at a remote distance where she could see them, but she felt no threat from them. She had always assumed that everyone had dreams about spiders, which meant she could assume she was normal and well-adjusted. But now she recalled reading somewhere that repetitive dreams had some deeper meaning. This was going to bug her, literally, until she did some research, but it would have to wait now that the NRC was going to allow West Isles to come back online. Things would be busy for a while.

When she entered the auxiliary building hallway, she could hear excited discussions coming from the radiation protection office. The news had already circulated that the FBI had identified a suspect and that the plant had been cleared for restart. She went to the doorway to listen in. Thumper, as usual, was in the middle of the room, talking the loudest.

"I told you it would be about sex—it's always about sex—it makes the world go round," Thumper said, trying to outshout the others.

"Who cares about sex? We've got the okay to go back online," said Jack, who had other things on his mind, like keeping his job.

Daryl (aka Opie) and Jerry were talking about how this would show those "idiot" newspaper reporters who were hoping for the worst so the plant would never start up again. Now there was real motivation to ensure this start-up went smoothly.

"Okay, everybody—hey Opie! Jerry!—let's get some focus here," said Cal loudly again, since Opie and Jerry continued to talk. Cal was the radiation protection supervisor for this shift. "I need your attention here!"

Cal could relate to the excitement. He was relieved himself that the murder had been solved, but now he felt the pressure to get back to work.

Lindy decided to hang around for the briefing since it might include some information on when the FBI would return. Also, there could be vital information that she should be aware of. Yeah, right, she said to herself, as if.

After a minute the room calmed down, and Cal was able to speak. "Operations wants to begin start-up tomorrow at 0700. We've got a lot of work to do before then. I'm going to ask some of you to work overtime. All work permits in containment need to be closed out—today. The mechanics and laborers are on the same schedule and will work overtime if necessary," said Cal, looking down at his clipboard.

Whenever the plant was down, crews did routine maintenance of pumps and valves in containment. It never hurt to be ahead of schedule on maintenance items, particularly on a system that was inaccessible when the plant was running. To power down due to a routine maintenance item that was overdue could be costly, not only because of the loss of power output but also because it would waste fuel. Nobody liked to see that happen. The most efficient nuclear plants run until the optimal amount of fuel has been used up, shutting down just before losing efficiency due to the buildup of power quelchers. (By-products of the fission process absorb neutrons and therefore lower the power output, quelching the power.) Although large maintenance projects such as inspecting the condition of the steam generators were usually saved for planned outages, several smaller projects had been started when the West Isles plant was taken off-line. Because the decision to power back up came unexpectedly, several of these jobs had to be closed out as quickly as possible.

"Ingalls, you've got the primary system auxiliary supply pump upgrade, on the minus-20. I heard the mechanics were just about done yesterday, so it should be a quick job—in and out by noon. And watch the removable contamination—they may generate some airborne."

"No problem, Cal, I'll keep them in line," Ingalls said authoritatively.

He had seen Lindy enter the room and hoped that she noticed him. He said hi as he left the room to get ready for the pre-job safety meeting and to get dressed out. Lindy nodded in return and moved out of the doorway to give him plenty of room to get by. Lindy found Fred Ingalls to be on the creepy side and avoided him as much as possible.

"Thumper, I need you on the pipe penetration job at ground level in containment. I guess there was some question about the packing around the penetration for the letdown line. Pretty high dose rate area, therefore I will help you with the safety review—give me about twenty minutes." Cal thumbed through the paperwork on his clipboard. It looked like he had one more job to coordinate.

"Milo, I need you on the job to finish up the safety injection pump upgrade. Again, a high rad area, as you are aware. The mechanics weren't happy with the previous work they did. You were there. The previous doses from the work done last week were pretty low, so you can handle this one alone."

"Milo can do," said Milo. Such a gift was all Milo could think at the time. Now he needed no excuse to get back into containment. Destiny was in play. The injection pump was located in containment near the location of the emergency core cooling system valve that was of new interest to Milo. He had spent many hours studying the diagram of this system and reasoned that if he closed this one valve, it would not be identified until the reactor reached 50 percent power, when the reheater pump would be needed. This should give him enough time to get in position to complete the malfunction of the other systems that he planned to disrupt. People for a Safe World would be very happy with what he had planned. There would be such a disruption of safety systems and concern for a loss of control of the reactor that it would guarantee passage of the proposition to shut down West Isles. And Milo was certain this would show those senior scientists at People for a Safe World that the effects of electromagnetic fields on people are real. They will have to take his manifesto to the public then, he thought. All he needed to do was swing by the waste gas decay tank room and pick up the cheater bar that he had left there. Milo found that he did not have enough strength to turn many of the larger valves in the plant. Several weeks ago he had made a copy of the key to the waste gas room, and nobody had noticed that the key was missing from the radiation protection key cabinet for a day. While he oversaw the mechanics working on the safety injection pump, he would take care of the valve. The mechanics wouldn't notice him gone for a few minutes.

Lindy waited for a mention of the FBI, but there was none. She decided to head to the control room to see what news they had.

The control room staff was busy getting ready for start-up the next morning. Although all the reactor operators had been repeatedly trained at the simulator on how to do a start-up from zero percent power, four operators were going over each step in the procedure in detail and discussing who would manage which systems. Two other operators appeared to be getting ready to do some more system walk-downs. Even though many walk-downs were completed for the investigations last week, they had to be done again because the technical specifications required they be done within twelve hours of each start-up. Lindy found Marcus Laiden sitting in his office with the technical specification manual on his lap.

"How you doing, Marcus?" asked Lindy.

"Great, I think." He had a lit cigarette hanging from his lips as he talked. Lindy noticed another smoldering butt hanging precariously on the edge of the ashtray on Laiden's desk. She reached over and rubbed the cigarette out before it created a bonfire.

"Marcus, you are an accident waiting to happen. Most people know they should only smoke one cigarette at a time. You know, these things are gonna kill you one of these days."

"Yeah, I know. I've got Lydia constantly on me to quit. I promised her I would. So how are you doing?" Since Marcus and Chris were good friends, Lindy had spent quite a bit of time with Lydia Laiden. She had liked being Chris' girlfriend. She felt it gave her a little better status at West Isles. It had been a nice side benefit to being with Chris, and now it was gone.

"Hear you are dating an FBI agent now," said Marcus. Lindy couldn't believe that even Marcus was in on the grapevine. Wasn't he too busy to listen to gossip?

Lindy said, "Rumors only. No truth to it—you should know better." Lindy expected the next person would have her engaged and maybe even married. Then it occurred to her that Chris might be the grape doing the gossiping.

"Oh, too bad. Sounded like a good thing," said Marcus, distracted.

"They are all good things," said Lindy, giving up on trying to distance herself from the single woman stereotype. "But not exactly for me. I hear you've gotten the word that we can start up tomorrow? Have you seen any of the feds here?"

"Yes, we will begin powering up tomorrow at 0700. I'm just going through the tech specs and making sure I haven't missed anything. With my luck, there may be some loophole where I need to, I don't know, maybe contact the county coroner and let him know that no other corpses have been found. Some of these requirements are beyond sensibility."

"I can believe that. So, maybe you will have a day without the FBI breathing down your neck?" said Lindy.

"No such luck. I have them arriving at 1300. Got a briefing with them and management. Good thing they pay me well."

"Oh, well, I will let you get back to work," said Lindy, backing out of the office.

Marcus at first appeared not to notice her leaving, but then he said, without looking up, "Your FBI friend will be coming to the meeting."

Chapter 24

LINDY WALKED OUT OF THE control room into the main hallway and immediately stepped back against the wall to avoid running into a group of mechanics, all dressed out in Tyvek. Their rubber boots made squeaky noises on the concrete floor as they walked down the hall. A few looked weathered and walked heavily, clearly in no rush to get to the step-off pad to enter containment. Others were younger and had restless looks; their eyelids opened up just a bit more than normal. They walked with lively steps, filled with a somewhat uncontrolled energy, bopping their heads around to face the older workers, firing off questions about the job they were about to do. The older workers kept walking at the same pace, sometimes ignoring the questions, sometimes answering, but clearly being very tolerant. They were once like these young pups, being trained themselves by some old coots. It appeared that the group was heading to a job that required work on a safety system in containment and would involve some training. These were usually the toughest jobs at the plant and required the most experienced workers. Not only would they need to perform quality work, they also had to do it fast and safely while working in a high radiation area. These highly paid workers were essential to the nuclear power business.

Thumper was dressed out and walking behind the group, apparently the safety escort for this group. He stopped near Lindy and said, "Sure you wouldn't want to take my place, Lulu? Gonna be fun—have some newbies in training—they'd probably rather see you strip down afterward than me."

"Thumper, you are very kind to think of others," said Lindy

sarcastically. "No, thanks." Lindy wondered who had told him about Maisie's nickname for her.

"Okay, but don't say later I didn't give you an opportunity to, do I dare say, show your exhibitionist side? I hear you may be short on action lately."

Lindy didn't say anything. She just gave him the finger and turned to walk off in the other direction. Chris Sievers was walking toward her. She hadn't seen him since the containment entry and wondered if he saw her gesture to Thumper, a little embarrassed to have been caught being bested by that lowlife. She used to confide in Chris about how frustrating it was to work with a bunch of chauvinistic pigs, and undoubtedly she hadn't been as strong in his presence as she always tried to appear at work. She was now beginning to understand why people say you shouldn't sleep with coworkers. On the brighter side, she found her house to be much more comfortable now that most of his things were out. It had to be something about spending years in tight quarters on those submarines that made Chris load up the house with stuff. Lindy had constant bruises on her legs and arms from bumping into furniture stacked so close together that a circuitous route was needed to get from one end of the house to the other. Lydia Laiden had the same problem and said that she wouldn't let Marcus do that to their house. Only their garage was packed tight.

"Andrews," said Chris, looking a little uncomfortable himself as he met up with her.

"Sievers," replied Lindy. Let him be uncomfortable. She had tried to make it work and wasn't going to feel intimidated.

They stood there for a few seconds, both avoiding a dead-on stare, waiting for the other to speak, but there was nothing more to say.

"I'm going to the control room," Chris finally said.

"Good. Good for you. You do that," said Lindy, using her motherly voice. Now that was awkward, she thought as she continued down the hall. It was going to be strained for a while.

Lindy went down the elevator and walked through the controlled area to the security building. At security she walked through the portal monitor and threw her badge and dosimeter in the drop-off bin, waving to the security guard standing at watch. She had some time before Sawyer returned, if he returned, so she headed toward the dosimetry trailer in the parking lot. She had yet to get through all those dosimetry reports from the outage.

She saw several cotton puff webs floating in the breeze out in the parking lot. She didn't remember seeing this many last spring. Lindy opened the door and walked into the trailer.

"Hi, Lindy. What's new?" asked Dottie. Dottie was the only one in the dosimetry office today. Jane had taken the day off.

"Things are bustling over there. Start-up begins tomorrow, so all the last-minute work needs to be completed before containment is buttoned up."

"Good. I'm glad to be going back online. It will really be a relief. I did issue some finger rings earlier for one job, but otherwise it's been quiet," said Dottie.

"Thank you."

"No problem," said Dottie, and then, as if she couldn't hold back, she continued, looking over the top of her glasses. "I hear the FBI will be back today."

Uncanny—how did Dottie and Jane get their information? I should have just asked Dottie when McMillan and the others would return and not bothered going to the control room. "Yeah, I heard that too. But I don't think they will be needing dosimetry."

"But maybe they will need other things?"

"Dottie, you and Jane are going to make me crazy. What do you know and how do you know it?"

"I'm sorry, Lindy, but you are like an open book. We were hoping McMillan would return. He seems like such a nice man."

Lindy was exasperated by the lack of privacy. She wasn't sure whether to tell Dottie that McMillan had called and mentioned dinner. Maybe it would make the situation worse. But then again, Dottie and Jane would find out sooner or later through their many sources. Maybe if she tried the best friend approach and begged for secrecy, Dottie would feel obligated not to share the information with others. Besides, Lindy was pretty excited about his call last night and really wanted to share it with someone.

"He seems to be an okay guy. We might be going out to dinner if he has time. But I wouldn't want that to get around, you know how people are. Of course, it may not happen."

"I think it will. I didn't tell you, but he asked about you the last time he was here getting dosimetry. Wanted to know if you were single."

"Really?"

"Really, girlfriend," said Dottie.

Dottie had worked with Lindy for two years and knew that Lindy had the habit of regularly underestimating herself. She and Jane had talked about it on several occasions, and in truth, Dottie could not understand why Lindy didn't understand her assets. It wasn't so much a lack of confidence, because they could tell that there was something more underneath. Jane and Dottie sensed that Lindy believed she didn't deserve better. It was subtle, but it appeared to be a pattern in her relationships. She seemed to just float along, going with the flow and becoming attached to whomever came along without giving much thought to whether the relationship was good for her. Jane and Dottie had agreed that Chris Sievers was a self-centered jerk, and they had just about thrown a party when they heard Chris had moved out. This McMillan guy seemed like a much better match for Lindy, but both could sense that Lindy was holding back. They had secretly agreed to encourage the relationship whenever they could. McMillan hadn't really asked about Lindy's marital status—he was too focused on the job. What Dottie and Jane actually did was go out of their way to tell McMillan that Lindy was knowledgeable and could really help him on this case. They were the ones who suggested that Lindy would be the best person with an overall knowledge of plant systems. They had bragged about how smart she was, how she could solve dosimetry problems that had stumped others. Sensing that McMillan was all about getting the job done, they made sure that Lindy would be his go-to person. It had worked, as evidenced by their dinner together a few nights ago. Now it was time to keep the relationship going.

"Oh, well, that's good, I mean, he seems ... malleable," said Lindy, a little surprised that Sawyer would be asking about her.

"Malleable? What are you thinking? He's not Play-Doh! You don't need to mold him into something other than what he is." Dottie shook her head, knowing now how Lindy got the nickname Lulu.

"I mean, he seems like he is flexible to fitting in."

"Hey, you are hot! You don't need a flexible man! Who wouldn't be interested in you?"

"What? Where did that come from?" Lindy said, shaking her head, wondering why Dottie felt the need to give her a pep talk. "I don't know what to think, but right now I've got work to do."

"I don't know what else I can do to make you understand ...," continued Dottie, but Lindy had already left the room.

Lindy was feeling overloaded and went into her office and sat down in front of the stack of paperwork. *He asked about me! Why did she do this to herself—getting all excited just to be let down?* She set out to review reports to keep her mind occupied and let the hours pass. If he had time for dinner, she probably wouldn't know until later in the day.

The dosimetry report for David Worth was on top of the paper pile, where she had left it the night before. She looked at the report with its unusual data record of low-energy gamma exposure, but nothing in the report gave any clue as to the cause. She pulled out the manufacturer's manual on the dosimeter Worth had worn and checked at what point the badge would separate out the low from high-energy gamma rays. The dosimeters were designed with several phosphor chips about the size of tiny pills. The phosphor material easily absorbed the energy from gamma or beta or neutron radiations. When the phosphor is later heated up by the dosimeter reading service, it releases the stored energy. The released energy is then measured in a special reader and compared to calibration records to assign a dose to the person who wore the badge. There were several dosimetry services that specialized in providing quality data for power plants across the nation.

Lindy rose from her chair and grabbed an empty coffee cup from the edge of her desk. She needed to think. And pacing and coffee usually helped. Dottie had left, but there was a fresh pot of coffee made. *Thank you, Dottie!* Now, what was going on with Worth's low-energy gamma exposure? What did it mean?

The dosimeters used at West Isles had three separate phosphor chips. The first was completely open to air because the cover had an opening that allowed the chip to measure all types of radiation, including beta radiation. Beta radiation can be stopped by a thin piece of paper, so any covering over the phosphor chip would prevent it from reaching the phosphor. The second phosphor chip was covered with a thin layer of Mylar that blocked beta radiation but still allowed the absorption of low- and high-energy gamma radiation. The last chip was covered with a thin piece of lead, which eliminate both beta and low-energy gamma radiation. With information from the three chips, one could calculate the separate exposures to beta, low-energy gamma, and high-energy gamma radiation. A separate neutron badge was needed for neutrons and was only issued to employees who worked around the reactor vessel or spent fuel. Federal law required that every worker's dose be tracked and records kept indefinitely. Dosimetry records were treated like medical records. Federal law imposed yearly limits on worker exposure. If a worker approached the limit, they would be put on office work until the end of the year. If the yearly limit was exceeded, which occurred occasionally, it required a detailed investigation, usually followed by large fines from the NRC. The federal limits were low enough that any short term adverse health effects would be impossible, although there was some increased future risk for cancer.

Now, why were there low- and high-energy radiation readings? Lindy continued to circle her desk, sipping her coffee. The answer to that question involved more theoretical atomic physics, which was not Lindy's expertise, but what mattered to Lindy was that if you can determine the energy of the gamma ray or beta radiation, you can identify the element, whether it's cesium, cobalt, or any other radioactive element. In the technical manual, Lindy found that the amount of lead in the third window would shield any gamma radiation energy higher than 580 kiloelectron volts (keV). Lindy knew that radioactive cesium had a signature energy of 661 keV, and cobalt was a lot higher, with an energy over 1,000 keV. This meant that these two nuclides could not have caused the dose measured in the low-energy window, and therefore David Worth went somewhere in the plant other than the containment building during the month. Cesium and cobalt were everywhere in containment, and since his badge measured less of these elements, he had to have gotten the low-energy dose somewhere else. Lindy stopped in midstride and plopped back in her chair.

She went down the list she kept handy on her desk of low-energy gamma emitters that might possibly result from the breaking up of the uranium atoms in the fuel. She eliminated most gamma emitters for lack of abundance and others for having a short half-life. Either of these traits would mean the gamma emitter would have little chance of causing a reading on anyone's badge. One of the last radionuclides on the list, radioactive krypton, caught Lindy's attention. She couldn't remember exactly what energy was characteristic for krypton, but she did know that krypton-85 was very abundant and had a fairly long half-life. She pulled out a reference book from her shelf, and lo and behold, it had one gamma at 514 keV. Bingo. This was probably the source of the exposure. Krypton is a gas, so it would become airborne instead of accumulating on surfaces in the containment building. It was produced when the uranium was fissioned in the reactor; over time, it leaked from the fuel rods into the primary coolant water. The krypton gas created when the plant was at power was collected from the primary coolant through an off-gas system and then pumped to a waste gas decay tank located in the radwaste building on the minus-20. The tanks were pressurized and could hold trillions of atoms of radioactive krypton. Three tanks were available, allowing one or two to be off-line to allow the krypton gas to decay for a year or so. This ensured that radioactive releases to the environment were reduced. When the tanks were full, the radiation level would be very high, so the room was locked to prevent inadvertent entry. If David Worth had gone into this room, it would explain the low-energy dose on his badge. The cause could still be a read error or a damaged chip, so further investigation was needed. Lindy decided to call the RP manager to check on any work done near the waste gas decay tanks.

"Jensen here."

"This is Lindy. Got a question for you. I found some funny readings on David Worth's dosimetry, you know, the dead guy?"

"What kind of results?" Jensen had done his time in dosimetry and was well aware of what a funny result could mean, and this interested him. He had also been in many meetings with Maddog lately, and any information that could help the investigation and keep him out of his office was a good thing.

"His reported low-energy gamma dose for May was much higher than the dose from high-energy gamma emitters."

"That's odd."

"Yeah, I don't see this kind of result often. The dosimeter would measure anything lower than 580 keV, which means the dose was not received from being anywhere in containment. It may be an error. But to be sure, I need to know if there were any radiation work permits issued for work in the waste gas decay tank room and whether Worth was on that RWP."

"I don't know, but I'll get right back to you with that information."

Al Jensen hung up, and Lindy went back her records. Maybe someone else has a similar dose report. Lindy quickly went through each record, looking only for low-energy gamma readings. After several minutes, she found another dosimetry record that had the low-energy readings: Milo Parker, a radiation protection technician.

Al Jensen called back, but he had surprising information. There was no radiation work permit issued for the decay tank room for the month of May, which meant there might be another explanation for the dose report.

"But get this," said Lindy, "Milo Parker has similar readings."

"Really? Does Osman's record show a similar dose report?"

"No, it doesn't, but that doesn't necessarily mean Osman didn't kill David Worth. Maybe Worth did a job with Milo Parker somewhere in the radwaste building?"

"Let me call you back. I'm going to find Milo Parker right now." Al Jensen hung up the phone so fast that Lindy was left listening to the dial tone.

A couple minutes later her phone rang again.

"Um, damn," said Jensen, "Milo went home at noon. He's switching to the nightshift and won't be in until tomorrow late afternoon. I'll try calling him at home when I get a chance. Thanks, Lindy." It was past noon already? The hours had flown by.

Chapter 25

IT WAS AFTER EIGHT O'CLOCK, and the only patrons in the restaurant were those who planned to stay and enjoy the band that would be arriving soon. Lindy and Sawyer were seated at a table on the deck outside the bar area. There was one light near the entrance to the bar and a lit candle here and there on the tables. White Christmas lights were strung around the deck, occasionally crisscrossing on a tree located beyond the deck. Crickets could be heard in the distance over the music coming from the bar. The slough was nearby, and the fresh smell of wet dirt permeated the air. There was a slight chill to the air arising from the slough, which was perfect for Lindy—she liked it on the cool side when having a drink. Roadhouse was the neighborhood restaurant and bar, one of the few restaurants near the power plant, so Lindy expected to see familiar faces. It could not get much better than this for a local hangout as far as she was concerned. It beat any high-rent party club in Los Angeles, she believed, although she had never been to such a place.

"This should be a celebration tonight. Sawyer McMillan has solved the mystery!" said Lindy.

"Yes, I believe drinks all around are needed!" said Sawyer. He looked around and laughed. "Even though it's just the two of us. It's been a long week, but looks like things are coming to a close."

"How's your case against Carl Osman shaping up?"

"It's coming along, but we still have some holes to fill. I heard that one of the managers at the plant said you were following up on some unusual dosimetry radiation readings?"

"That is correct, Mr. FBI Man. Much improved on the jargon by the way," said Lindy. "Didn't seem to take you long to get the nukespeak down."

"Glad to hear you approve, Ms. Radiation Safety. Am I going to have to wait for dessert before I hear what you have on the radiation dose?"

"No, no, not at all. If it was anything conclusive, we would have gotten the information to you right away. But the jury is still out on whether this will amount to anything. If you recall, you had requested that I look through the dosimetry records, and as I was looking through the last months reports ...," said Lindy, being sure to emphasize that the work was being done at his request, "I found that David Worth had an unusual dose report for the month of May during the outage."

McMillan leaned forward, ready to speak.

"But ..." Lindy raised her finger in the air, and McMillan leaned back.

"Always the 'but' word."

"We are not sure if it has any relevance yet. We—meaning, if you didn't know, the radiation protection manager and yours truly—need to interview one of the RP techs tomorrow who has a similar dose report. Doesn't mean much on the surface, and I'm betting it will be just a read error or some other mundane reason such as 'laundry machine abuse.'"

"At this point anything and everything could be helpful, laundry abuse or not. We still can't put Osman at a location near the murder site. If there was something in the records showing David Worth and Carl Osman were in the same location, that would be very helpful."

"Unfortunately, the data shows that possibly this RP tech and David Worth were in the same location, but not with Osman. Sorry, but it could be coincidence."

"Ah, I guess my career rests on the mercy of a very intelligent and beautiful woman to figure out the clues?"

"Yes!" Lindy had to laugh. How absurd was this conversation.

"Okay," said McMillan, raising his glass of whiskey, "here's to Lindy's brains!" Lindy toasted with McMillan. It was the first time he had called her by her first name.

She caught him looking at her over his whiskey glass. It was a look she had never seen before, and it made her cheeks hot. Or maybe it was just the whiskey. They plunked their shot glasses on the table.

"Seriously," said Lindy, "we will follow up on the unusual dose readings, but it could be nothing."

"Understood. Hey, I wanted to ask you about the article in the *Valley Sun*. Your previous discussion about the emergency safety systems seemed to leave out a little possible accident consequence called the China syndrome. Based on the article, it sounds like that was a big omission on your part."

"Ah, come on! You can't believe everything you read in the paper!"

"Is that so? A bubbly mass of uranium sinking to the middle of Earth doesn't seem that far fetched considering the multiple concerns you all have about keeping the fuel covered and cooled. The reporter did his homework, Lindy. The story was picked up by the *Washington Post*, for God's sake. My boss called from DC about the story."

Lindy felt her stomach flip flop. "That's not good. I gather the story was picked up by other papers too? Very unfortunate. That's all we need before the election—national attention."

McMillan continued. "I'm sure the China syndrome discussion has raised some interest, but my boss was more concerned about the leak of information. Somehow the reporter knew that a safety system in containment had been misaligned. Someone from the plant must have given out this information, because all the public relations offices agreed to keep this information under wraps. He's asked me to check with Mr. Cahill about whether there are any actions that can be taken to assure there are no further releases of information," said McMillan, clearly concerned.

Lindy thought about possibilities for a second and then said, "Everyone knew about the misaligned valve found on the ECCS system. Anyone could have leaked the information."

Lindy and McMillan sipped their whiskeys in silence.

"I hate to bring it up, but there's something else bugging me about that article," Lindy said finally.

"There's more?" Sawyer asked, motioning to the waitress for another round. Lindy frowned at him.

"Afraid so … You know, Margaret Colliers asked me to meet the reporter with her. She said they were hoping to put a softer face on the power plant and decided a woman would be more sympathetic. Do you remember from the article the part about how power plant workers are risk takers and don't mind putting their health in jeopardy? That was how he interpreted my statement that I wasn't worried about the amount of radiation exposure I had received while working at the plant."

"That did seem to be a bizarre statement."

"That's not exactly what I said. I said the danger to my health was very small, but somehow that got left out, and he only remembered that I told him life is risky. I guess I shouldn't have confused him with scientific facts. That was the only problem we had with the article, and I should give the reporter credit for a least getting the other radiation facts correct."

"Sounds like you did pretty well to me. First time talking to the press?"

"Yes. Not easy at all."

"True. I try to leave the interviews for others. But, seriously, about the China syndrome ..."

"I mean, really, McMillan, one valve out of alignment does not mean the China syndrome could happen, even if the China syndrome were possible."

"So you are saying the China syndrome can't happen?"

"Of course not. It took a lot of designing to get the fuel configured so that the chain reaction would be maintained and produce power. Once the fuel melts, it's no longer in the perfect configuration, and so the chain reaction will be lost. I'm not an expert on fuel, but I would guess melted fuel would look initially like a bubbly mass, but eventually the fuel would cool, starting with the outer edges, preventing it from moving through the Earth. It would be a nasty mess, but not an uncontrolled disaster. Besides, fuel melted at Three Mile Island, and it was all contained. The China syndrome only works in movies."

Sawyer looked lost in thought for a moment. "I see. But you've got to admit, it did seem to have some truth to it."

"Yeah, I imagine most people believe the China syndrome could happen, and probably even worse things." She sipped her drink, knowing this was the case. McMillan ordered another round.

"So, tell me, what got you into this business of radiation safety? It seems like an odd career for a woman."

"I never planned on working in a nuclear power plant. It just kind of happened. In college I was working on my biology degree and happened to take an introductory class in nuclear engineering. Engineering didn't interest me, but the effects of radiation on the human body really caught my interest. I switched to health physics, and a couple of years later I found myself at the power plant. It is my niche, though. I am very comfortable in this job. It's hectic, but what job isn't?"

"It's an interesting place. It has its public service angle, which never occurred to me before."

"I see you have picked up our commitment to making power for people?"

"Yes, not something I've come across in many other businesses."

"Besides clean water, can you think of anything more important to people than electricity to power their homes? It's a given that electricity is always available, and most don't think about having to live without it until there's the occasional blackout. That's when we find out most people think it's a right and demand that their service be restored. We in the power business know that power availability is what keeps the United States at the top of the heap, so a few angry customers once in awhile are no big deal."

"Thank God you are working hard every day, because I don't like to work in the dark," said Sawyer. His words were slightly slurred, and his face softened. He stared intently at her.

"Are you trying to flatter me?"

"Yes, of course. I like you. You are very entertaining in a nerdy sort of way."

"And I should take that as a compliment?"

"Of course."

"Then tell me something about you. How'd you end up at the FBI?"

"I always wanted to be in law enforcement since I was little kid. We used to play Alcatraz as kids. You know, the game where the girls are the criminals and you have to catch them and take them back to jail."

"Only the girls were the criminals?" Lindy could picture him being the leader of a bunch of dirt-covered boys playing prison guards.

"Yes, they were escapees and we had to capture them. And for being bad escapees, we took our squirt guns and had the girls open their mouths, and then we would aim for that thing that hangs in the back of the mouth. The girls loved it."

"Oh, my God, that is hilarious! How old were you?" Lindy was laughing pretty hard, imaging him as a kid.

"I don't know, maybe eight or nine. It only tickled if you actually got a good shot in. Mostly the girls got pretty wet in the face."

"And this is what made you become the FBI agent that you are today? Did you put this on your résumé when you applied?" laughed Lindy.

"Yeah, sure. That would have gone over well."

"This is very interesting. I would have never guessed this about you."

"Yes, that's the story I usually give people," said McMillan in a more serious tone, "although I had other motivations later in life for going into law enforcement."

"Like what?" Lindy hoped he would continue, although she got the feeling that he really didn't want to talk about it. The alcohol seemed to have loosened him up, appearing to make him say more than he planned.

"Well, it was because of what happened to my dad when I was a teenager. Some con men swindled him out of the family farm back in Wisconsin. It still makes me mad today that those assholes got away with it."

Lindy sensed that there was more to the story. "It must have been hard on him."

"Yeah, he's okay though, now. He worked hard and bought some other land that keeps him busy. Too busy, in fact. My brother has had to take over some of the chores because Dad's getting too old to keep up."

"I'm glad everything worked out for him. So, I guess if we are going to eat we should be looking at these menus." said Lindy. Time to change the subject.

"You know, Lindy, I'll be leaving soon and going back to DC."

She lowered her eyes. "Yes, I know."

"I like you. A lot," he said. "I've never met a woman like you." He reached for her hand.

"You're smart, funny, and dedicated to your job. I love that about you."

Lindy bit her lower lip. "Now you're embarrassing me."

"No, I mean it. Look," he said, holding both her hands, "when this is over, I'll be back. There's nobody waiting for me in DC. I'll be back."

"Nobody in DC?" Lindy found that surprising.

"Nobody in DC. I did have someone, but it ended. I guess I didn't pay enough attention to her. Obviously, my job takes me out of town quite a bit."

"I can see that."

"Yes, it does, and it seems she had a hard time being alone. Not much going on in her life to sustain her while I was gone. But she moved on. It didn't take her long to find another man, from what I hear."

"You sure you are okay with that?"

"Yes, I am okay with it. She was a predatory woman who had no life of her own and was feeding on me. It sounds harsh, I know. I guess it took me awhile to see that, but I eventually did, and I'm happy the relationship is over. And I am happy that I met you."

At this point, the last thing on Lindy's mind was ordering food from the menu she had in front of her. She also didn't care who might be watching and was thrilled to find that the right chemistry was happening between them. They had been talking so long that the band was starting to warm up, and more people had arrived. It was getting crowded and loud.

"It looks like the band will be playing soon. Do you know of a place with a little more privacy? I'm not that hungry anymore," said McMillan.

"Uh, privacy?"

"You know, a place where we can be by ourselves."

"Really, now? Is this an FBI special request?"

"Yes, I believe so."

"Okay, then. There's an overlook for the creek just down the road." And before Lindy knew it, McMillan was in his car following her there.

It was dark, and no one was around on the desolate dirt road, but you could hear the rush of the creek underneath the bridge. They stood together on the bridge, staring down in the direction of the rushing water. McMillan put his arm around Lindy's waist, pulled her close, and began to kiss her. There was no other purpose to the kiss, except to feel her lips against his. It was one of the most memorable moments that Lindy had every experienced.

Later, Lindy and Sawyer spent the night together, and neither of them would forget the kiss at the creek.

Chapter 26

When Lindy got to work the next morning, she heard that things had gone so well that plant start-up had been moved up to 0300. The situation at work was taking a turn for the better. It was amazing, too, the change she felt just knowing that Sawyer enjoyed being with her. They had discussed the fact that a long-term relationship could not happen and agreed to keep their relationship as friends with benefits. She knew that this was all she could expect and decided it would be better to move on to looking for someone who could be more available. It was just a matter of not thinking about him. That should be easy.

Upon Lindy's arrival, Dottie immediately filled her in on the latest. All was going well so far. Now that they were heading back to power, the dosimetry workload would slow, and they could use the time to catch up on reports that had been put aside while the issuing of dosimetry took priority. Jane was doing some of that work and seemed rather preoccupied and not as talkative as normal. Did she already know that Sawyer and she had spent the night together? Did Dottie and Jane have spies at her house? Did Jane think she looked different? She certainly felt different and hoped it didn't show. Lindy didn't want to get into the relationship that she had agreed on with Sawyer. Dottie and Jane were guaranteed to lecture her that she was giving the milk away for free.

Before they could say anything, Lindy grabbed the dosimetry reports for the Worths, Carl Osman, and Milo Parker and headed to Al Jensen's office in the auxiliary building. Jensen had cleared his schedule to allow time for them to go over the results together. Sawyer thought he would be at this meeting since it could bring more evidence against the assumed killer, Carl Osman. Lindy pretended not to care whether he would be there or not when he mentioned it to her.

Lindy found Jensen in his office along with one of the other radiological engineers named Don Ryder. Jensen waved her in as he talked on the telephone.

When he hung up the phone, Jensen said, "We are at 40 percent power already. All systems go. Okay, Andrews, show us the reports." Lindy put all four reports on Al's desk so that Ryder could look on.

"Here's David Worth's report. Clearly, some low-energy gamma." Ryder and Jensen nodded in agreement.

"And here's Carl Osman's report—no low gamma." Lindy pointed to the report and then showed them the fourth report. "But see here, Milo Parker has a similar low gamma dose reading." Jensen and Ryder took a few seconds to look at the reports just in case Lindy missed something.

"Interesting," said Ryder, "did you talk with the dosimetry service and see what the energy spectrum showed?"

"I did. Low gamma radiation was indicated, and there were no other indications of water or heat damage to the phosphor."

Ryder continued, "How about ..."

Before Ryder could finish his comment, a message came over the loudspeaker that made them all stop and listen.

"Attention! There is a medical emergency in the minus-40 aux building! On-shift medical team is needed immediately! Repeat, there is a medical emergency. Medical team, report immediately!"

Jensen's phone rang. He grabbed it quickly, listened briefly, then hung up and reached for his hardhat.

"Get some hardhats and come with me. We are going to the minus-40."

Lindy and Ryder followed Jensen to the staircase. Jensen took the four flights of stairs submarine style by sliding down the handrail. Ryder followed suit, but Lindy wasn't as good at sliding, so she skipped as many stair steps as possible to keep up.

When they reached the minus-40 level, they found several people standing around in a circle where three motionless workers lay on the concrete floor. One man was lying on top of the other two. About five feet off the ground there was a high-powered drill; the drill bit was buried in the wall, holding the drill body horizontal to the wall. The drill's cord was disconnected from a nearby extension cord that snaked around a corner, probably connecting to a power source that was out of sight. Thumper was talking.

"I don't know what happened, but I wouldn't touch anything yet. Earlier these two guys were setting up for work here. I was down the hall when we heard someone yell 'Help!' I came here, and this is what I found. I think Charlie was the one who yelled." Charlie was a mechanic who looked like he was the last to go down, since he lay on top of the other two.

"We should try and revive them, now!" said the nurse who was on the medical team. She started to reach for Charlie.

"Wait!" said Marcus Laiden, who had just arrived from the control room to see the situation firsthand. "Why did these guys go down? I believe Charlie was trying to help and somehow was affected also. We need to know so no one else is hurt! I hope it's not an airborne problem." An airborne concern had not occurred to anyone before. This made several who were watching start to shuffle several feet back from the scene.

"Was it an electrical short in the drill?"

"One-ten wouldn't do this. It'd have to be high voltage!" said one of operators. "But from where?"

"I just checked where the extension cord was plugged in—it's only 110!" shouted a worker from down the hall.

Laiden looked again at the drill lodged in the wall and the dangling cord hanging from it, disconnected from the extension cord. Then after a few seconds the scene made sense to Laiden. He now understood what had happened and immediately ordered safe actions. "Nobody touch that drill! You, you, and you! Grab their feet and drag them away from the drill! It's safe to work on the men once they are moved."

Thumper and the other operators grabbed the men and dragged them about ten feet down the hall. The nurse quickly checked for a pulse on Charlie's neck and bent over to check for breathing. She started to pump Charlie's chest and yelled, "Get the defib unit! Now!"

The other two men were in a similar state, not breathing and no pulse. One emergency medical technician had started mouth to mouth. Jerry, the radiation protection technician, was hunched over the third man, looking a little nervous about how to proceed. A radiation protection technician was always assigned to the emergency medical team on every shift. Although he had been to the medical training yearly, he had never before had to do CPR on a real person. Thumper saw his hesitation and went over to assist.

Instead of watching the medical staff, Laiden kept his eye on the drill in the wall. Laiden was thinking about the possibility that these men would not make it. This would mean he will have lost three men during his watch, and he would take it personally. While Laiden was a commander on his submarine, he had never lost a man. The emotional feelings he was experiencing were new to him. He considered what would be expected of him if the worst happened. He was not looking forward to the personal visits he was going to have to make to family members. He assumed that would be standard procedure for civilians also.

Lindy saw his pensive look and then asked, "So what happened?"

Marcus didn't look at her. "Behind this wall is a 250 kV electrical cable run. I believe Train B, the one that's juiced."

Lindy was beginning to understand.

"Whoever was drilling probably died the instant they hit the cable. And I'm guessing the assistant probably tried to get the other's hands off the drill and was electrocuted also. People are good electrical conductors."

Lindy could only nod in agreement, too numb do anything else.

"And then I'm guessing Charlie came along and thought all he needed to do was unplug the drill, which was safe to do because of the insulation on the cord. However, he must have accidentally touched the drill body when he went to help the other two guys. Damn! Damn! Damn it! Why weren't these guys using their heads! Who authorized this work?"

"Sir," shouted the nurse to Laiden, "Charlie is breathing again! It looks like he's going to make it."

Laiden turned and nodded, but then he looked for the status of the other two men. The emergency medical technician working on one of the men shook his head slowly, which indicated the resuscitation was not working yet. The defib unit had had no effect. Laiden saw that the medical technician was in an automated mode while performing the resuscitation, obviously knowing that it was probably fruitless, but he continued anyway. However, it was a different situation for Jerry and

Thumper. They were whispering desperately to the man to wake up and breathe, pushing harder on his chest, hoping to make him come to. Laiden realized it was probably going to be hard for Thumper and Jerry once they realized their efforts were for naught. It was common for people who do not succeed at CPR to suffer depression afterward, because of the shame they felt, thinking that they possibly had done something wrong and allowed a death to occur. Realizing that CPR was often ineffective, the safety class now included a session on how to cope with the loss of life and a discussion on the reality that CPR may not be successful in preventing death. Laiden thought that Thumper would be able to handle the loss, but he was concerned about Jerry, knowing that he tended to take things personally. Laiden would ensure he talked with the two sometime soon to let them know that they had done the best they could.

In the meantime, Laiden got on the phone in the hallway and called to the control room to get the power trains switched to allow the drill to be taken out of the wall. He had one of the operators check the technical specifications manual just in case there was a time limit on when authorities needed to be called. He didn't expect that start-up would be delayed, since this was an accident unrelated to safety systems, but one never knew. To give himself a little time alone, he took the stairs back.

Chapter 27

Tom Mietner pulled up in a rental car in front of the home at 12344 Green Creek Road. Mietner was glad that the rambling ranch house was on a large acreage lot that allowed several dozen yards of space between neighboring houses. The lots in this part of town were called horse properties because owners tended to have enough land for one or two horses. But most properties only had manicured rolling green lawns, weeping willows, and an occasional duck pond.

Mietner had made a small effort to disguise his looks by wearing a fake mustache and glasses and adding some gray coloring to his hair. He hoped the time he spent at this home would be limited, making later identification by the family less likely. He had thought long and hard about how to get out of doing what Milo had asked him to do, but could not find an alternate plan that worked and also left him out of the picture. He figured the likelihood that he would be identified later was slim and had even made sure to get a rental car from an out-of-town office using phony identification.

He rang the doorbell.

"Can I help you?" An attractive woman in her thirties with short brown hair opened the door wide. She had rubber gloves in one hand and must have been in the middle of cleaning when the doorbell rang.

"Yes, miss, my name is Darren Wood, and I'm with the local redevelopment committee. We are surveying homeowners in the area on the current redevelopment plans that the town is proposing. I was hoping you could take a few minutes away from your busy schedule to answer a few questions. And hopefully get your input on the development plans?"

The woman hesitated as if thinking whether to let him inside. Then she shrugged.

"Sure, come in. Let me get my kids settled down, and I will be right back."

"Thank you," said Mietner. He stepped in to the hallway and took a quick look around for the telephone and found it was located nearby in the family room. Good location, Mietner thought, centrally located where he could keep an eye on the family and the telephone at the same time.

Chapter 28

When Milo arrived for his shift, several hours had passed since the electrical accident. He found the security staff preoccupied, even though this would normally be a slow time for them. He overheard the security guards talking excitedly and asked what had happened. Milo had just missed the coroner leaving with two bodies, they said grimly. They told him about the drill in the wall. He shook his head in total agreement with them about the tragedy, but internally he had different thoughts. People were too one-dimensional to think that a sudden high-voltage bolt was the only way electricity caused death. The imperceptible deterioration of their cells from electromagnetic fields should be their real concern. Milo thought this accident was a sign that his mission was divinely inspired. How often did something this significant happen? God had sent this message as a reminder of how important it was for people to hear his manifesto, a reminder of how oblivious people were to the real danger. There was no better time than now to remind people of the real danger. He was emboldened to continue the mission by the news of the accident and headed quickly to the auxiliary building to proceed with his plan. He still had two hours before his shift started.

Milo went to the auxiliary building, and instead of reporting at the RP office, he stopped by the lunchroom and rifled through the drawers. Once he found what he was looking for, he headed to the control room. When Milo opened the door, he saw three reactor operators monitoring the control boards. They were intent on watching for problems while the plant was powering up. If anything were to go wrong, it would happen now, so full concentration was required on their part. Once the plant was at full power, the control boards would stabilize, and fewer changes and events requiring intervention would occur. Milo went straight into the shift supervisor's office and shut the door.

"What's up?" asked Marcus Laiden when he saw Milo enter.

"Nothing much, except that the human race is going to die," said Milo, "unless I stop the stupidity."

Marcus Laiden looked at Milo with surprise. "Sure, we all are going to die, eventually, both stupid and smart people." Laiden looked narrowly at Milo. "Maybe you haven't heard. Two guys were killed today. Electrocuted."

Milo came around Laiden's desk and stood where the reactor operators out in the control room could not see what he was doing through the glass windows. He then opened his jacket and showed the knife he had in his inner pocket.

"Just do what you are told and nothing will happen to your wife and kids."

"What? What are you talking about?"

"Look." Milo waved a Polaroid picture at Laiden. "Yes, it's your house. If you do what I say, nothing bad will happen."

"What?"

"Don't do anything to alert your operators, or there may be consequences to your family. I need you to come with me and assist me in saving the world."

"And why should I do that?" Laiden smirked. "That looks like a kid's knife to me."

"Call your wife." Milo gave him the phone receiver.

Laiden hesitated but then dialed the number for his house. "Hello, Lydia? What's going on? Are the kids okay?"

Laiden listened for a while then hung up the phone with a sense of resignation. "What do you want me to do?"

"I want you to act like nothing unusual is happening. Don't be a hero for the company—the safety of your family depends on that. If you do good, your wife and kids will be fine. Let's leave together. Tell the others that you need to check something out with me."

Milo and Laiden left the control room with hardly a glance from the operators, for they were intently focused on the next step of the start-up procedure and were now approaching 50 percent power, at which point another round of safety checks would be due.

Chapter 29

LINDY WAS NOT NEEDED IN the aftermath of the electrical accident. She returned to her office and told Jane and Dottie about the accident. It seemed unreal and untimely that the deaths should occur right when they were in desperate need of getting back online and making power. The election was only days away, and every effort to show the efficiency of the plant was important to bolster the voters' faith that the plant was a stable facility, ready to provide years of cheap power. Jane and Dottie were relieved to hear that the accident would not halt the start-up.

Sawyer had not come to the plant, and she had no messages waiting for her at the office. Something must have come up. She was disappointed. Should she give him a quick call to say hello? Nope, she decided. She didn't want to appear needy. She wondered if he'd heard about the accident.

Although she had not gotten the opportunity to talk with Al Jensen about the dosimetry results, it did not seem to be urgent considering they had the suspect in custody. Jensen had a lot on his plate today with the accident and the start-up in progress. But just in case, Lindy spent several hours going through the dosimetry reports from the outage once more and entered the data into the dosimetry record database as she went along. Finally, she had them all entered. David Worth and Milo Parker were the only ones with the unusual low-energy gamma readings. Lindy was surprised to see some dose reported for Norm Callaway, however. He very rarely went anywhere in the plant where he would be in a radiation area. Norm hated leaving his instrument calibration lab. Lindy decided to ask Norm about it during her next visit to the auxiliary building. She also wondered if Jensen would remember to interview Milo when he came in for his shift in a couple of hours.

Just to be thorough, Lindy decided to check the log-in history for the dosimetry system. The system kept a record of all entries and updates, the times they were made, and who made them. She and the managers were the only ones that had access to the log-in history. It had been a helpful feature on past occasions when lazy radiation protection technicians had decided to "radio in" their surveys, which was jargon for technicians making up radiation measurements for the survey report instead of actually taking the measurements. Uncovering the sham reports required a correlation of information in the security database where card key entries were recorded. If the security database did not show that the workers had entered the facility area to be surveyed, then it brought into question whether the surveys were actually conducted. It was pretty easy to check since every survey had to dated and signed. Two radiation protection technicians on backshift had been fired after it was found they had never gone to the rooms or areas that they had supposedly surveyed.

Lindy pulled up the log from the terminal on her desk and began reviewing the log-ins, starting with the most current. Everyone had to log in on a dosimetry terminal at the start of a job and before entering the controlled area. Exits from the controlled area were also listed, including the dose that the person read on their pocket dosimeters. Many personnel made entries on radiation work permits. Occasionally various members of the radiation protection staff would make inquiries about radiation work permits and queries on dose limits and training records. Lindy scanned several pages of entries and then came across a query that seemed unusual. Now, why would Milo Parker need that information? Looking up someone's home address was not a routine query. The dosimetry technicians regularly accessed personal information to mail dosimetry records to someone's home, but Milo wouldn't need it. And why Marcus Laiden's address? They weren't friends as far as she knew. Milo was pretty much a loner. Milo Parker, with the low-energy dose similar to the dead guy. What's the connection? Milo would have access to the key to the waste gas decay tank room that was stored in the office, but why would he and Worth go there? Lindy remembered Wade, her friend from the training department, talking about Milo's nutty fear of electromagnetic fields and about all the questions he had about the emergency core cooling system. The valve that was misaligned in containment was part of the core cooling system. Lindy had a bad feeling about this. Milo had always seemed a little off to her, and now that she thought about it, he seemed capable of doing something really stupid. She grabbed the phone and dialed the control room. Hopefully Marcus Laiden had an explanation.

Lindy listened to three rings, which seemed like an eternity. Come on! Pick up! Finally someone answered, but it wasn't Laiden. "Where's Laiden?"

After hearing the explanation, Lindy quickly hung up and looked for Sawyer's mobile phone number. She dialed the number and prayed he would answer.

"Sawyer!" said Lindy, relieved to reach him, "you need to get here right away! I think something terrible is going down."

Chapter 30

SAWYER MET LINDY AT THE security building. Security guards in swat gear and carrying rifles were standing by, ready to escort them to the control room. The plant was in a high security alert because the shift supervisor, Marcus Laiden, could not be located. No one was allowed to roam freely in the controlled area under this heightened security threat level. Once it was determined that the shift supervisor was missing, nonessential staff were escorted off the site, and only essential personnel remained. The grounds of the controlled area were desolate, making West Isles seem like a hostage in limbo.

"I should have figured this out sooner," Lindy told McMillan as they ran to the auxiliary building, "and we may be too late. The operators are now starting to power down because there have been some problems."

"Never too late," said Sawyer, his face like stone. "What's going on?"

"It's Milo Parker—I don't know how I missed it. He's got to be the one who killed David Worth! He's the RP tech with the funny dosimeter reading. He's taken Marcus, the shift supervisor, somewhere in plant. I think he's trying to cause a LOCA—loss of coolant accident."

"Why?"

"I don't know why he's doing it. But everything points to him. I think he's crazy enough to do something stupid. He's got this wild theory that electromagnetic fields are killing people and that he's the only one who understands the problem. I'm guessing he believes that if he causes an accident it will get everyone to pay attention to what he thinks is the real problem."

They reached the control room and entered. Lindy saw Cahill, Clemons, Sievers, and several systems engineers and operators. For a second she wondered why Sievers was there but then realized he would be taking over Laiden's job as acting shift supervisor. The men were all standing over a large diagram, pointing at different locations. One of the systems engineers, Santelli, was talking: "... and it looks like this new valve in containment has been locked out of service and caused the first ECCS alarm. Water volumes have not changed. I don't see any big concerns at this point. We should be able to shut down without a problem."

"Good," said Cahill.

"As long as there are no other surprises," continued Santelli, looking like he was expecting a response from Cahill, but none came.

Lindy realized that Milo Parker had access to containment when the plant was powered down. He would know which systems had been cleared, and since they would not be checked again, he could make hazardous valve alignment changes on those systems. The problems the reactor operators were currently encountering could be chalked up to Milo Parker.

"Clemons, report!" yelled Cahill.

Harry Clemons, the security manager, stood up with a wheeze. "Milo Parker entered the controlled area at 1708 hours. No suspicious activity at entry, except a few guards did tell him about the electrical accident. No other security area entries before the time he kidnapped Laiden, which was at 1732 hours, as reported by the control room operators. Since then, the last card key entry for Laiden was at the minus-40 level of the auxiliary building. Parker has not card-keyed anywhere, so I assume he's tailgating. We have only a few card key locations below the minus-40. There's the resin tank room, the aux building radwaste sump tank room, and the secured electrical rooms. None of those have been actuated. We've got Team Alpha situated at various locations throughout the building. No visuals yet. Your previous order still stands?"

"Yes, take out Milo Parker if given the chance," said Cahill without remorse.

"I've got Krause, my best shot, located in the aux building. Ex-sniper for the army and …"

Before Clemons could finish, an alarm went off that made the engineers and operators look with concern at the control room annunciator panels. There were four different sounds that were used for the alarms. This allowed the operators to quickly differentiate between levels of concern. Some alarms were a low chirping sound and were used for plant conditions that did not require immediate attention. Some sounded like a clang of a bell, which indicated a higher level of concern. But the latest alarm that caught everyone's attention sounded like a siren. The siren alarm meant a system critical to reactor safety was out of specification and required immediate attention.

With a burst of energy, Sievers moved to the control panels and shouted, "The pressurizer water level is rising! How could that be? Vinnie, what's going on? Is there a fix? What power are we at? Somebody! Get me the pressurizer system description! Riley, what's the RCS temp? And pressure?" Lindy could see his cheeks reddening. His eyes darted in all directions. Sweat covered his brow.

As he spoke, other alarms went off, some less important than others. The two control room operators were busy watching the annunciator boards as the number of flashing lights increased. Santelli scrambled through the manuals on shelves.

"Reactor coolant system—pressure, flow rate, temp, all normal!" yelled Riley.

"Pressurizer level still rising! PS-211 alarming! Valve PS-211 has opened! Opening valve PS-329 recommended at 97 percent—we're not there yet! Currently 72 percent," said Vinnie. Opening PS-329 would allow water to drain from the pressurizer. Vinnie was correct that they had time to hold off on opening the valve.

"Got it!" said the engineer as he threw the system diagram on top of the low bookcases near the panels.

"Where's PS-211?" asked Sievers, standing over the diagram.

The systems engineer closely scanned the large intricate engineering graphic and then put his finger where he had found the valve. He looked at Sievers with an expression that visibly showed that he had bad news to share. "It's a back-up control valve for the pressurizer, accessed only at the remote control panel. It adds water automatically to the pressurizer when actuated."

Although she was not following all the discussion on the system valves, the mention of the remote control panel sent a chill down Lindy's spine. The location of the remote control panel was known only to the operators and a few security and engineering staff. The panel was a miniature version of the control panels in the control room except it only had safety system controls and switches. It was a fail-safe backup system to shut down the reactor in the unlikely chance that the control room was inaccessible or taken over by hostile parties. It overrode the systems in the control room. Laiden knew the location of the panel and would have a key to enter the room. Lindy wondered what Milo had done that made Laiden willing to take him to the remote panel.

When he heard the news, Sievers' face lost some color, and at that moment Lindy felt sympathy for him. It was all in his hands to make the decisions to ensure the reactor shutdown occurred in a safe manner. Although they were powering down, the reactor pressure and temperature were high enough that serious consequences could still occur. His boss, Maddog, was in the control room. Even though Maddog was the plant manager, Sievers had ultimate authority in the control room. This actually made sense and was a good arrangement, in that the authority lay with the person trained to safely operate the plant and not with the one who was in charge of making the money.

"Leggit, get your ass to the minus-60—the remote control panel room—now!" said Clemons, yelling at his radio to one of his security men.

"Anyone? Any ideas on how to proceed? I could use some help here," said Sievers. Santelli and the two operators, Vinnie and Riley, were looking through the system descriptions and watching the alarms, but they did not have any suggestions on what to do in the current situation. They had not been tested on this scenario at the simulator. Direct tampering with systems was not usually considered; the focus of training scenarios centered on equipment malfunctions and human error. The remote control panel hadn't been used in an accident scenario that anyone could remember, and most people had long forgotten that the remote panel even existed. The reactor engineers thought of the panel as useless overkill, one of those pieces of required equipment that the regulators put on the reactor design under the pretense of adding additional safety features. This supposed safety feature was turning into a conduit for disaster.

The operators were also hesitating to recommend the use of PS-329 to control the pressurizer volume, since this was the valve that was involved in the accident at Three Mile Island some five years earlier. That was the only nuclear power plant accident of any magnitude in the United States, and it still carried a stigma of death for the public, despite the fact that no one had been hurt in the accident. As it turned out, if the operators at Three Mile Island had left the pressurizer level alone, the system would have self-corrected and the power plant would be in operation today. The operators had caused the damage to the fuel by manually draining water from the reactor coolant system. It was a great quirk of fate that if the Three Mile Island plant had been left to itself, it would have shut down safely. Clearly, no one at West Isles wanted to repeat that accident.

"Let's think, people," Sievers said, taking deep breaths. "We've got a few minutes before the pressurizer goes solid. Let's not panic."

He paused and then said, "Riley, where's Scooter?"

"I don't know, boss."

"Get him on the phone! Now!"

Scooter, also known as Scott Winfeld, was the oldest and most experienced reactor operator at West Isles. He had to give up working in the control room because he had so many facts and figures in his head. The details overwhelmed him and paralyzed him from taking action when required. He had been moved to support staff many years ago but was always relied on for the tougher questions.

Clemons' radio crackled, and everyone heard the report that the door to the remote panel had been jammed and couldn't be opened. They were not sure if anyone was still inside, and the guards had not come across Milo or Laiden on their way to the room.

While the commotion continued, Lindy thought about what she would do if she wanted to cause an event that would attract national attention. Certainly causing the reactor core to overheat and possibly causing fuel damage would be news in itself, but to really cause hoopla, there had to be some danger to the public. And to have danger to the public, there would have to be a release of radiation from the containment building. That would not be easy to accomplish. The containment was designed to withstand high pressures, and it was designed to be isolated from the surrounding buildings as much as possible. But there had to be entries to the auxiliary building for systems that maintained the primary coolant system chemistry, among other things. All the openings through the thick concrete walls were located together in rooms, usually referred to as the penetration rooms. The steam lines were an exception to this. The steam lines had to exit the containment building to deliver the steam to the turbine building. Causing damage to the steam lines would be difficult. They were hard to access and very robust since they needed to withstand the superheated steam produced by the steam generators. Lindy thought that damaging some of the auxiliary systems would be easier for one individual, so she considered the possible locations and systems that would allow a release of the radioactive particles and gases that were currently contained.

The loss of coolant accident that could occur at this point wasn't guaranteed to happen with just the pressurizer system problem. It was a serious problem, but any increased radiation would still be contained. The backup safety system, the emergency core cooling system, would need to be compromised to get something that would really cause a threat to the public. And that was the system that Milo had been interested in during his systems training and the one where the misaligned valve had been found. Lindy had a guess as to where Milo would need to go to cause a release of radioactive material that could eventually be released into the environment. Although the levels of radioactivity released through damaging the auxiliary systems would not be lethal, it would be devastating to the reputation of the plant.

"Sawyer, I've got an idea of what Milo might be up to. Let's go. I'll tell you on the way."

Lindy went to Clemons on her way to the door. "We're going to check out a hunch. Don't let your guys shoot us, okay?"

Clemons nodded, and Sawyer and Lindy headed out the control room.

"Hold on. Need to get a meter," said Lindy, as she ran down the hall to the RP office.

When she returned, she said, "Let's go. To the minus-80." Together they headed for the auxiliary building elevator.

Chapter 31

THE LIGHT FROM A FEW caged lightbulbs on the walls just barely kept the hallway from being completely dark. The minus-80 level was rarely accessed since there were few systems down there that required frequent maintenance. There was a stagnant odor to the air. The lower levels were reserved for the dregs, and minus-80 was the final low point in the plant for collecting waste and spills. Because of this, it was also known to have some of the highest gamma radiation areas in the plant. Nobody volunteered to work on jobs at this level. The areas of interest to Lindy were the containment penetration wraparound rooms, where systems that had components in both containment and the auxiliary building were connected by penetrations through the eight-foot-thick wall. They were called wraparound rooms because one wall of the room was the curved exterior wall of the containment building. Containment penetrations were strictly limited to ensure the integrity of the containment building. If needed, the control room could close each penetration by issuing a containment isolation command, although some systems would need to remain open for emergency operations. There were pipe penetrations for such things as the containment sump pump drains, which removed any excess water seepage that might collect in containment. And there was a penetration for the chemical and volume and control system, known as the CVCS, and also a penetration for the letdown system. The CVCS allowed addition of chemicals into the primary coolant to control the acidity of the water or other parameters that needed adjustment. Acidic water would cause corrosion of piping and was therefore an important quality to control. The letdown system allowed controllers to bleed water from the cooling system or dilute contaminants. There were a few other minor penetrations, such as the small line that allowed reactor coolant to be extracted for analysis. This line went directly to a lead-lined room in the back of the chemistry hot lab. But the penetrations that interested Lindy now were the backup safety injection tank connections. These were part of the emergency core cooling system located in the east penetration room.

Sawyer followed Lindy down the hallway to the east penetration room, whose entrance was located on the left. Lindy stopped when she reached the door. They could hear a hammering noise, metal on metal, coming from the room. Lindy pointed at her meter in silence to remind him that the radiation levels would be high in the room. Then Sawyer pushed the door open, pointed his gun, and used his flashlight to survey the room.

"Look!" Sawyer said, pointing ahead of them.

"What is it? I don't see anything," Lindy said. She searched the darkness with her eyes.

"It's gone," Sawyer said. "I thought I saw someone." Whatever he had seen had fled into the back area of the room, out of sight. Lindy followed Sawyer as he carefully scanned the room, gun in front of him. He worked his way toward the back of room where a ladder was located. Whoever was in the room had escaped using the ladder. Lindy looked at her meter and saw the dose rate was high in the room.

"Let's get out of here. High dose," she said.

"But I don't feel anything different," Sawyer said. "Are you sure?"

"Of course, dummy," Lindy said, frowning. "You can't detect radiation through normal senses. You can't see it, smell it, taste it, feel it, or hear it. Trust me on this."

"Okay, okay, we're leaving."

Before leaving the room, Lindy checked around for damage to any piping. The banging heard earlier was severe, and water was collecting on the floor in the room. Lindy saw a broken pipeline the led out through a penetration in the containment wall, and water was pouring out the break. She quickly memorized the number of the valve located nearby. Lindy inspected the other piping and found that a bracket on a locked open valve was broken, meaning that the valve had been closed. Then Lindy moved quickly to the exit. Sawyer was waiting outside the door in the hallway. A lip on the doorway had so far prevented the water from leaving the room, but the level was rising quickly, and in a few minutes it would overflow into the hallway. Lindy decided not to mention to Sawyer that their shoes and pants bottoms were probably contaminated from the water on the floor in the penetration room.

Once they were together in the hallway, Sawyer asked, "Not that much dose, right?"

"No, not that high at all. You'll live," said Lindy, knowing that they both had probably exceeded their dose allotments for the quarter. What she found interesting, though, was that Milo had been in the room for far longer than she and Sawyer and had probably received a much more significant dose. Most people would be concerned about that, and it made her wonder what motivated Milo.

"Is Milo alone?" asked Lindy.

"Possibly. I only saw one person in the shadows, but I could have missed seeing Laiden. Milo may have already taken out Laiden if he didn't need him anymore."

Lindy considered that possibility. It sounded logical, because Milo only needed Laiden to open the remote control panel room. Lindy hoped the worst had not occurred.

"What now?" said Sawyer.

"Let me think. The ladder in the back of the room would have taken Milo back to the minus-60. If he heads back toward the remote control panel room, security will surely find him. So, if he's smart, he will go the other direction toward the fuel building, or he might choose to go the long way around to the turbine building." Lindy remained silent for a moment while she weighed the options.

"Wait! He wouldn't go to the turbine building! The electromagnetic field would be huge there! He must have gone to the fuel building!"

"Lead the way," said Sawyer. Lindy headed to the elevator.

Sawyer was now completely disoriented as to where they were in the facility. Lindy had gone a different way back to the minus-60, using a set of stairs at the other end of the minus-80 hallway. They encountered a security guard on the stairs, but fortunately he did not have a trigger finger, although he did have his rifle in hand and Lindy in his sights when they rounded the corner on the stairs.

"Halt! Don't move!"

Lindy was too surprised to speak. "FBI, McMillan! And Lindy

Andrews. Clemons should have mentioned we would be in the neighborhood!"

The man lowered his rifle. "Just wanted to be certain that you were alone first."

McMillan understood exactly his concern, having been in that situation before. "Sir, you are exactly right on that. Good job. Now, can you give us a status?"

"One patrol is still working on the jammed door at the remote panel—should have it open soon. But the control room is having some system leak issues. You would need to talk to operations staff about that. No sign of Mr. Parker or Mr. Laiden yet."

Lindy knew that Milo would have bypassed this location by using the auxiliary stairs. Lindy asked to use the security guard's radio and used it to relay the status of the damage done by Milo in the wraparound penetration room. Based on this information, Sievers in the control room arranged to send a repair team and reactor operator to open the safety injection tank valve and minimize the leakage from the other system. Sievers also arranged to have security staff meet Lindy and Sawyer at the fuel building.

When Lindy and Sawyer arrived at the entrance to the fuel building, there was no one there yet. Before entering, Lindy turned to Sawyer and said, "The fuel building is a large open space, and there won't be any cover once we enter. Do you have a plan?"

"Plan? Yeah, I have a plan! Shoot the son of a bitch!"

Lindy looked at Sawyer with concern. "One request, though. If I say don't shoot, will you hold back? There may be mitigating safety concerns with surrounding equipment."

"Such as?"

"Such as gas-filled tanks or plant safety equipment, for starters."

"Okay, okay. I will check with you before I shoot," said Sawyer hesitantly. Lindy could see that Sawyer was concerned about this. Shooting the bad guy had probably always worked for him before. "I don't want to, but I will."

Lindy smiled at him. "Thanks."

With that, Sawyer slowly opened the door, and Lindy cautiously looked over his shoulder. At first glance, everything appeared normal. Lindy glanced at the radiation meter located above the fuel pool, and it was not alarming. That was a good sign. As they stepped forward, they could immediately see the entire area inside the large building. In the middle of the building was a deep pool of water that had a cerulean blue color to it. From this angle they could not see the spent fuel located several feet under the water, nor could they see that the color of the water near the fuel was much more intense because of the radiation coming off the fuel, but it did slightly reflect on the concrete walls of the fuel building, creating an eerie ambience. The building had tall ceilings to accommodate the large crane that was used to move the fuel during refueling of the reactor. The spent fuel would be removed from the reactor in the containment building and then moved through the transfer tube into the fuel building and placed in the fuel pool for temporary storage. The spent fuel was highly radioactive and would be deadly if encountered without the shielding of water in the fuel pool.

Lindy knew that the water was a very good shield against the high radiation levels that were coming off the spent fuel. Being in the building presented no danger, as long as you did not enter the fuel pool. And, of course, it was vital that the water level remain high enough to shield the fuel. The water itself acted as a moderator and prevented the fuel from overheating, but it was also loaded with boron to absorb the neutrons.

Sawyer and Lindy cautiously walked in the open space around the fuel pool in the building, but they did not see or hear any sign of Milo. Lindy began to think that she had made the wrong call and that Milo had overcome his fear of electromagnetic fields and gone to the turbine building to escape detection. As they walked around the fuel pool, Lindy did not see anything out of order.

"I don't think he's here," said Lindy.

"Okay, where then?"

"He must have headed to the turbine building."

"Are you sure?"

"No."

"Well, let's go then."

Chapter 32

THE TURBINE BUILDING WAS WHERE electricity was made. When the plant was built, West Isles had one of the largest turbines in the world. It was the second-largest building at West Isles; containment was slightly bigger. Lindy occasionally visited the building because the plant ventilation system ran between the buildings and the radiation monitoring equipment for the vent was located in the turbine building. Otherwise, she would have no reason to go to the turbine building, because it was part of the clean side of the plant, for the contaminated water in the reactor coolant system was physically separated from the steam and water in the turbine building by several barriers. At some nuclear plants, contaminated steam and water would come in contact with the turbine, and therefore the entire turbine building and structures were in the radiation controlled area. But that was not the case at West Isles.

Lindy and Sawyer entered the south end of the building near the high-pressure turbine housing structure. The structure that housed the turbine rose about twenty feet above the walkway and was in a housing that mimicked the circular shape of the turbine fins. The turbine's steel fins were connected to a shaft. As the steam crossed over the fins, it caused the shaft to spin, which turned the generator; electricity was generated by massive magnets passing other massive magnets in the shaft. The turbine was in operation during shutdown to help extract heat from the reactor as it proceeded to zero power. At the same time, the turbine was still generating power. The noise level was thunderous and earplugs were required in the building, though Lindy and Sawyer did not have any. Because high radiation was not a concern and he had the gun, Lindy let Sawyer lead the way.

The building was well lit, and Sawyer cautiously stepped out, looking quickly in all directions with his gun aimed ahead of him. Not seeing any movement, he slowly walked past the turbine housing and other miscellaneous equipment and headed toward the generator. Lindy didn't think they would find Milo here, but it was the last place to check. She stopped for a minute to check her meter, and she was surprised to see that it was reading a few millirem per hour. She had expected it to be at background level in the turbine building, meaning zero, and she was curious.

At that moment, someone grabbed her from behind, put a knife to her throat, and yelled in her ear. "Hold it, or I'll cut you!"

Lindy froze. Sawyer was a few feet ahead looking forward and didn't hear the threat. She debated whether to scream, but decided against it since she wasn't sure she could get her voice to work. Better to act tough.

"Milo, what do you want?"

"Just stay with me and nothing will happen," said Milo as he walked her backward toward the turbine housing located in the center of the building. Lindy thought this was odd, because Sawyer would turn around any minute now to check on her, and then what was Milo going to do?

When Sawyer turned, he saw Milo and Lindy standing next to the turbine shaft housing. He walked back slowly, keeping the gun pointed at Milo. When he was a few feet away, Milo said, "Don't come any closer. Stay right there!"

Lindy noticed that Milo sounded tired and that he didn't have a very strong grip on her. His hand and lower arm were red and swollen. But what immediately concerned her was that Sawyer may take a shot, and that would be regrettable. She hoped Sawyer remembered her earlier request.

"Sawyer, let's be safe here, safety first," she said, hoping he understood her meaning.

"Yes, Sawyer, safety first!" said Milo. "What Andrews is trying to tell you is that if you shoot a hole in the turbine housing, superheated steam will escape and cut through both me and Andrews like butter." Lindy nodded in agreement. She wasn't sure if a bullet would stop in Milo's body or just head right through and damage the turbine housing.

Sawyer relaxed his arms and slightly lowered his gun. "So, what are we doing here, Milo? There's no way out for you."

"I know! Milo is not an idiot! This really shows how ignorant you are, though. Right now we are standing in an electromagnetic field that is slowly killing you, me, and your friend here. Every minute standing here is killing more of your cells than you would ever suspect, more than anyone would suspect. But Milo knows. He can feel it happening."

"Let's get out of here then. No reason for all this cell damage to take place," said Sawyer, trying to sound sympathetic.

Milo shook his head. "It's too late for me. Tell him, Andrews. Tell him the bad news about me throwing up several times on the way over here. Tell him what happens when you spend just a little too much time fixing systems in high radiation zones so that the world will know the real danger of electromagnetic radiation."

"What?" said Sawyer. He had no idea what Milo was talking about.

"What Milo is saying is that he has symptoms of acute radiation syndrome," said Lindy. "The first sign that you've received an overdose of radiation is when the cells in your stomach lining are killed, causing you to throw up. But Milo, there's still time! Even mild syndrome has vomiting. With medical treatment, you could be saved!"

"Yeah, right, like those poor people who were accidentally exposed in Brazil? They died slowly and suffered terribly—medical help only extended their pain. Not for Milo. No long, drawn-out suffering for Milo. Andrews, you and me are going to be specimens for the scientists. Milo estimates another fifteen minutes and you will be in as bad a shape as me due to the electromagnetic radiation coming off this turbine. They can use our bodies to show the world the real hazard of electromagnetic fields." Milo was smiling now, a sublime smile, knowing that he had just about completed his mission.

Lindy rolled her eyes to let Sawyer know that she thought that ridiculous. Sawyer took the cue to mean they had time to discuss some things.

"But nobody's going to know unless you live long enough to tell everyone," said Sawyer, trying to think of ways to get Milo to give it up and let Lindy go.

"Not a problem, Mr. Sawyer, Milo has friends. Right about now they should be releasing his manifesto, which explains it all and provides research that proves the fact. Milo is too smart for you."

"Yes, that's very smart planning on your part. What friends are those?"

"Oh, just some caring people who work for People for a Safe World. Milo explained his theory, and they immediately understood the problem and agreed that the people of the world needed to know ..."

As Milo talked, Lindy brought her foot up and kicked as hard as she could at his shin. In his deteriorated state, this made him let go of her and grab his shin. Lindy took off.

"Andrews, that hurt," said Milo, still holding his shin.

"Good," said Lindy, rubbing her neck where she had a slight cut.

"Okay, Milo, time to go." Sawyer leaned down and grabbed the knife and threw it aside.

"Wait. I'm not ready. Give me a minute, I'm very tired." Milo went to sit down, but Sawyer grabbed him by his arm.

"Well, then, maybe you have time to answer some questions while we let you rest? Why'd you kill David Worth?"

"David Worth? That jerk? Milo didn't kill him," said Milo, catching his breath.

Lindy had to jump in. "But you and he were the only ones with the low dose reading. You were together ..."

"Yeah, I was the tech covering a cleanup job he had, and I made him go with me to the waste gas decay room to hide the cheater bar. He didn't know that, though. He was so busy talking about how he was going to be rich soon, he didn't even notice Milo's detour," said Milo, bending over and groaning. Lindy looked quizzically at Sawyer, wondering if he was buying this story.

"But you did mess with valves for the emergency core cooling?"

"Yeah, it ... was part of the plan."

"Okay, we got to get going. People are going to want to talk with you," said Sawyer, seeing that Milo was not looking good at all.

"If you make me go now, I won't tell you what I did in the plant," said Milo, barely at a whisper.

"That's okay, I'm sure the operators will figure it out."

"No, they won't. Milo knows ..." and before he could finish his sentence, Milo began retching and throwing up massive amounts of

171

fluid. It wracked his whole body. Sawyer stood back to avoid the spray of liquid mixed with blood. The explosive release stopped for a minute, and Milo looked to Andrews and said, "Sorry." His body then retched one more time, but nothing came out and he collapsed.

By this time, two security guards had arrived, and one of the guards checked for a pulse and found none. The guard radioed back the situation to the control room.

Lindy had seen too many dead bodies this day and looked to blame someone. "Those damn bastards! Look what they did to Milo! They used him, those bastards. They knew he was crazy but used him anyway. They hurt people and don't care. Those sons of bitches!" She was just about to tear up when a call came in from the control room.

"Andrews, they want to talk with you," said Krause.

Lindy grabbed the radio. "Andrews here." It was Sievers.

"Lindy, we are still having some problems with the shutdown. Did Milo say what he did?"

"No, he died before he could. What could he have done?"

"Did you see anything unusual earlier?"

"The letdown line in the wraparound was busted."

"Knew that—what else?"

"It looked like the ECCS safety injection valve was closed."

"Fixed that! Anything else?"

"No."

"Thanks. If you think of anything to explain why the plant vent monitor is alarming, let me know." And Sievers was gone.

"That's strange. The plant vent is alarming ... doesn't make sense," Lindy looked up in thought and continued talking to herself. "The plant vent monitor is alarming. Why?" All Sawyer could do was walk alongside her, hoping that she would eventually share with him.

Lindy continued to talk to herself as she walked. "What did you do, Milo? The leaks caused at letdown would have vented to the radwaste building ... The fuel building goes to plant vent ... Milo, did you do something in the fuel building? Nothing out of order when we were there earlier," said Lindy to herself as she walked toward the control room. Then she turned to Sawyer.

"Do you remember seeing ripples on the surface of the fuel pool?"

"I don't recall."

"Where's my meter? Are you coming? We've got to check this out."
Lindy turned back to return to the turbine building where she last had
her meter. Hopefully, it was still operable after being dropped when
Milo grabbed her.

Sawyer followed, saying under his breath, "Do I have a choice?"

Lindy found her meter. It appeared to be working and still showed
a slightly elevated reading. "Let's go."

Lindy headed to the east end of the turbine building and went
up three flights of stairs that appeared to lead to nowhere but actually
aimed at a platform in the corner of the building near the ceiling. On
the second flight of stairs, she stopped and checked her meter. "We can't
go any further," she said.

"Why?"

"Look. Meter is going off scale," said Lindy. She turned on the
clicker volume for a minute, and Sawyer heard screaming fast ticks.
She turned it off.

"Oh," said Sawyer, "enough said."

"Very clever, Milo," said Lindy, almost admiringly. "Let's go. We
need to inform the control room."

Once in the control room, Lindy explained why the plant vent
monitor was alarming. Milo knew that he needed to have the public
in peril issue to get attention, but he really didn't have a way to force
the plant to release radioactivity at levels high enough to cause public
concern.

"Therefore, he did the next best thing," said Lindy. "He faked a
high reading. But it cost him his life. What was he thinking? He was
in the fuel building for just long enough to retrieve one of those highly
activated flow diffuser sections that were stored in the bottom of the
fuel pool. He had to have previously moved the flow diffuser section
to a location in the fuel building that he could easily reach with the
swing arm."

Metal baffle plates, called flow diffusers, were installed around the
fuel rods to diffuse or distribute water flow. Over time, the metal of the
diffusers becomes highly radioactive from the constant bombardment
of neutrons from the fuel, and when these parts needed replacement,
the old parts were stored in the fuel pool along with the spent fuel. A
diffuser section was small enough for one person to carry.

Lindy now addressed the operators. "The radiation monitor in the fuel building probably alarmed when he pulled the diffuser section out of the pool, but considering all the other alarms occurring at the same time, I imagine you overlooked it since the alarm would have ended once Milo left the building with the diffuser section."

Those in the control room nodded with understanding, but Sawyer was still confused.

"And he took the diffuser section and placed it near the plant vent monitor. The radiation detectors that monitor the air leaving the plant vent stack would pick up the gamma radiation coming off the diffuser, but you all in the control room would assume that the elevated readings meant that radioactivity was being released to the atmosphere. You would have to assume that the wind was carrying a radioactive plume into the atmosphere."

Lindy added the following additional information for Sawyer's benefit. "It appeared as though a major release of radioactive material was in progress, and it would have been assumed that Milo had found some way to cause a leak from containment. That high reading we measured on the stairs leading to the plant vent monitor was due to the diffuser section that Milo had placed near the monitor. It was causing a false reading on the plant vent monitor."

The control room operators, and especially Sievers, looked relieved. They had halted any more damage being done to the emergency core cooling system but had been puzzled by the vent reading. The team that was preparing to investigate the vent monitor now turned to plan out how to retrieve the diffuser section without getting dosed like Milo did. Sievers had been on the telephone telling the regulators about the situation. He was about to declare a general emergency because the readings on the vent monitor were so high. Nearby residents would have been hearing sirens and packing their bags if Lindy hadn't discovered what Milo had done.

"Carrying that metal plate is what killed Milo?" asked Sawyer.

"Yes, lethal levels of radiation," said Lindy, for once being able to use that phrase in all seriousness. She saw a look of relief cross Sawyer's face.

"Ah, did you think that being in the wraparound room was what killed Milo?"

"Well, yes," said Sawyer.

"And you thought we were next?"

"Well ... I didn't know."

"We got some dose, but nothing like what Milo got."

"Good to know." Sawyer looked relieved.

"Do you believe Milo didn't kill David Worth?"

"I don't know what to think. Milo mentioned that Worth was preoccupied with the idea he was going to make a lot of money. During my interviews, there was some talk of a few operators getting involved in some kind of investment that seemed a little shady. Mike Dire, the operations manager mentioned his involvement during his interview," said Sawyer, "but I never followed up on it once we found Carl Osman. Since Osman and Worth were friendly for a while, we could ask Osman, but he won't talk with us off the record. We were working on a deposition date."

"I don't think Milo had any reason to lie. He already knew he was a dead man," said Lindy.

"Yeah, I will need to look at my notes. Maybe there is something I missed."

"I heard some rumblings about investment schemes, but I usually stayed away from those discussions. Norm Callaway once mentioned he could help me make a lot of money."

"Norm Callaway? The instrument guy? I ruled him out since he said he never went into containment during the outage."

"But he had dose on his dosimetry! He must have gone somewhere in the plant to get that dose. Maybe he hasn't been all that truthful. You know, I think we ought to go to his instrument lab and check something out."

The auxiliary and support building hallways were empty except for the security staff stationed at various locations. Lindy reached the instrument calibration lab first and switched on the light. She headed straight to Norm's desk, located toward the back.

Lindy looked around, and then started opening draws and cabinets. "It's got to be here somewhere."

"What are you looking for?" asked Sawyer.

"Aha. Here it is." Lindy had found the neutron meter that Norm had retrieved from her the other day and put it on Norm's desk.

"It's destroyed," said Sawyer.

"Yeah, it's in really bad shape. Somebody had to work hard to get it into this shape. Can you tell if there is blood on it?" asked Lindy.

Sawyer took a close look at the instrument. "Yeah, this could be dried blood. So you think Norm did it? Killed Worth with this meter?"

"Maybe so. Norm was very agitated that I took it from the lab. It appears he lied about going into containment … and then there's the money scheme angle."

"Yeah, next to love, money is the best motive for murder," said Sawyer, reaching for the telephone. "Let me make some calls and get this looked into. Would Norm be at home?"

"Well, he wouldn't be here—he's not essential staff."

When Sawyer got off the phone, Lindy said, "We better go back to the control room and let Maddog, er, I mean Cahill know what we found."

"No, what you found. You do have a knack for this detective stuff."

"Thanks."

Chapter 33

LINDY SAT DOWN, THOROUGHLY WORN out, and she wasn't sure she would be able to stand up again. The adrenaline that was racing through her veins earlier had run dry, leaving her drained and exhausted. She found watching the people in the control room relaxing and pleasantly nostalgic. She watched Maddog and Sievers in the supervisor's office going over with the resident inspector what was needed from here on out. Earlier Maddog had told her "Good job"—an unbelievable moment for Lindy—and it had surprised others that he could actually say something encouraging.

She looked at Sievers again. Strangely, she felt no surge of emotion, no rapid heartbeat, no longing to be surrounded by his arms. He had ignored her for weeks. Yes, he was a good-looking, take-charge guy, but his treatment of her had been shabby, to say the least. Dottie had told her she'd seen Sievers and Ashley, a cutie from accounting, whispering in one of the back hallways. Lindy was not surprised. The last time they had a serious conversation, Lindy had asked him why he needed to move on. Wasn't having a relationship with one woman enough? His response was surprising. He said that it was like unwrapping a present: it was new and exciting to date different women. Well, it sounded as if Sievers had found some new presents in the accounting office. Yes, Lindy had just about had enough of Chris Sievers.

Across the room, two control room operators had resumed their level of typical activity, checking a gauge here, flipping a switch there. The plant had reached zero power and now was in cool-down mode. The operators were also depressurizing the reactor coolant system.

Lindy then watched Sawyer on his mobile telephone over in a corner, most likely talking to his bosses. He was a helluva guy, she mused. Fearless. Exciting. Good looking. A risk taker. Just the kind of guy she was looking for. She sighed and wondered if there could ever be any future for them and figured what would be would be. At this she felt her old self talking, as if things were out of her control, that she would just end up where the wind took her. At that moment, she decided to decide her future. She wasn't sure whether Sawyer was the man for her, but, damn it, she was going to make a decision. If she decided she wanted Sawyer, then she was going to do whatever was necessary to be with him. But she would think about that later. Now she was just happy to be sitting down.

Clemons had given a briefing earlier and said that once the guards got the remote control panel door opened, they had found Laiden lying on the floor, knocked out. It appeared that Milo had hit him pretty hard on the head. He was currently at the nursing station. There was some discussion of airlifting Laiden to the local trauma hospital just to be sure he got tests done as soon as possible. The nurse thought his head injury was not life threatening, although he could use some stitches.

Clemons also provided a summary of what had happened at the Laiden residence. Mrs. Laiden had called the control room after her captor left the house in a rush. He had kept Mrs. Laiden and the two kids on the couch while he paced in front of them with his gun out. She was a bit shaken from the experience of being held hostage, but what really overwhelmed her was her anxiety about her husband. Word was that she wouldn't get off the phone to call the sheriff until Clemons repeatedly assured her that Laiden was fine. Sheriff's deputies were at the house now, and they had called in a description of the car that the stranger drove away in.

Al Jensen came into the control room. As he walked by Lindy, he pinched her shoulder and smiled. Others followed in for the briefing that was about to begin. The room filled up to the point that there was only standing room. Lindy continued to sit despite the fact all she could see were butts in jeans.

Maddog began the briefing. "Today will go down in the history books as a victory for America. We have shown the world that nuclear power is safe, even when there are those who try to destroy the plant. You should all be very proud of what you accomplished today. You were tough and stayed confident in your knowledge even though all the signs pointed in a different direction as to the condition of the power plant. Good job, all of you. Without power, a country is weak and therefore vulnerable to its enemies. Electric power drives the economy and fuels productivity. There are some who think that we would be better off without nuclear power, but they are wrong. Nuclear power is the future—it is your children's future, and today you made that future more secure. Good job, but let's get back to work. A lot needs to be done!"

The speech was corny, Lindy thought, but she knew Maddog firmly believed in what he said. Lindy looked for Sawyer to see his reaction but couldn't see him through the crowd. She would ask him later. The operations manager began going over the status of the plant, and his slow drone of acronyms and valve numbers made Lindy's eyes shut, and she fell asleep sitting up.

The rustling of the staff heading for the exit was the next thing Lindy heard. She was embarrassed to realize she had fallen asleep and wondered how long she was out. As the last few filed out of the control room, Sawyer came over.

"Catching a few zees?"

"Did anyone notice besides you?"

"I think Maddog may have noticed," said Sawyer, laughing.

"Damn!" said Lindy, disappointed in herself. "What's that saying again? One 'aw shit' erases ten 'attaboys'?"

"Something like that. I'm sure Maddog understood."

"Do you want to grab a burger?' Sawyer asked, motioning toward the door. "I'm starved." His blue eyes bore into her.

She murmured, "I'd love to," and took Sawyer's outstretched hand.

Lindy and Sawyer were heading for the door when Thumper walked in carrying a meter. When he saw Lindy, he turned around and yelled down the hall, "I found 'em. In the control room."

He came back in and said, "Sorry, Mr. McMillan, I need to survey your feet. Want to sit for a minute?" Both Lindy and Sawyer sat down and raised their feet for Thumper. He had the volume up, and when the frisker passed the bottom of Lindy's shoe, the ticks increased significantly. The same occurred with Sawyer.

"I thought so! You've tracked contamination all over this plant, young lady. Mr. McMillan, you are not to blame. You didn't know any better," said Thumper.

Lindy rolled her eyes at Sawyer but was too tired to bother saying anything in response.

"Okay, both of you, to decon—now. We'll start with taking off your shoes and go from there. I wouldn't be surprised if you've gotten it all over your clothes, Lulu," said Thumper, who didn't stop talking at Lindy as they walked down the hallway with him.

"It might be even necessary for you both to take off all your clothes … and just to be sure … I better do the whole body survey since I am the best. You know me, leave no stone unturned …"

*　　*　　*　　*

"Art speaking," said Art Bigsbee, who was at his office working on paying the bills for the organization. He had an open bottle of whiskey and a plastic glass that was partly full.

Art listened for a second. "Tom, good to hear from you. How's everything?"

"Oh, I'm sorry to hear that. I hope your mother does better soon," Art said, "I guess that's why you haven't been by. The kids were missing those great lunches and morning donuts."

Art took a sip of his whiskey as he listened. "Well, that is bad news for us. It's going to be that long? Well, maybe things will turn for the better soon. Uh, by the way, is it possible to get some more funds from you? Maybe you could mail a check. I was just looking at the books, and we are a bit short on the rent again. A few hundred would do."

Art cringed at the response he heard through the earpiece. "Okay, I understand. Of course, we can hold on for a short while. … Yes, but it can't be long. And you know, the election is getting close—this is a crucial time—I would hate to lose the momentum we've gained. Maybe you can talk with Rackerby's people about some funding? … Great. Well, thanks for all your efforts, and thanks for the call. I wish your mother well." Art felt like slamming the phone down but held back. It looked like he was going to have to borrow from his personal savings account again. It was always a tight situation trying to make ends meet. You'd think more people would be interested in supporting this important cause. He took a big swig from the plastic glass and went back to his paperwork.

Chapter 34

BY THE NEXT DAY, THE story was circulating that Norm Callaway had been arrested for the murder of David Worth. Two FBI agents went to his home to ask him a few questions. The stress of the situation must have been too much for him, and when he found out they had the neutron meter with blood on it, he broke down and confessed. David Worth had invested his life savings with Norm and then had a change of heart about the investment. When Worth asked Norm for a refund, Norm made up some excuses, but Worth didn't buy it and threatened to complain to the authorities. Norm asked for a few days to round up the cash, but he had a problem. Norm had used Worth's money to pay off some of his other investors. His pyramid plan was falling apart, and after five good years of staying ahead in the stock market, he had finally fallen behind, and all the money was gone. Norm decided the only thing he could do was to get rid of Worth. With him no longer demanding a refund, he might be able to recover his business.

Norm knew Worth's work schedule and had gone into containment with the excuse of delivering a meter to a technician who was on a job. He inserted his card key at the containment hatch entrance but made sure he didn't put it in far enough for it to register. The security guard did not notice that the familiar click and blinking red light had not occurred and casually approved Norm's entry. Norm wasn't sure what exactly he was going to do, but he thought it best not to have a record of his entry. He found Worth in containment and again tried to explain that it would take awhile to get his money back. Worth was livid, realizing that Norm had probably lost his money. Worth reached for Norm in anger, and out of fear, Norm swung the meter he was holding and knocked Worth to the ground. Norm was astonished at his strength as he stared at Worth sprawled on the concrete floor. Quickly he dragged the body back to a hiding place but removed Worth's security badge and dosimetry. He then cleaned up the blood with some decontamination towels that he picked up on his way into contaminant, and upon exit, he carefully threw them away in the fifty-five-gallon drum, being sure that the bloodstains could not be seen. He used Worth's badge to card-key out.

Once Norm's story came out, the radwaste staff researched their records and found that the drum was on its way to a low-level radioactive waste site. The FBI made arrangements to have the shipment returned and later retrieved the bloody decontamination towels. When it looked like Carl Osman was going to take the blame for his action, Norm stayed quiet, but he did say he felt a heavy weight lifted when he confessed. He didn't have a reason for why he didn't get rid of the meter, but he did say he damaged it so it was beyond use.

During the backshift, maintenance staff repaired all the damage done by Milo in the wraparound room. They worked overnight to drain the water that had collected, and laborers helped the radiation protection technicians decontaminate the floors and walls of the room. The many hallways that Lindy and Sawyer had tracked contamination into were also cleaned and cleared for normal usage. After that, the welders removed the damaged section of pipe and welding in a new section. Quality assurance engineers did their nondestructive testing to certify the welds, and now the emergency core cooling system was in a test mode to ensure system integrity. The highly radioactive diffuser plate that Milo had left at the plant vent had been remotely transferred to a lead container that was placed nearby at the base of the stairway. Once the cover was placed, the dose rate was significantly decreased in the general area. The next step was to get the container back to the fuel building. The entire project was taking quite a bit of time due to the planning required for the weight and size of the lead container. Maintenance hoped to have the diffuser back in the fuel by the end of shift.

Marcus Laiden had been released from the hospital early that morning. Reports said that he had a hell of a headache and a concussion but was otherwise okay. The FBI and NRC inspectors would be heading to his home later that day to interview him.

Reactor operators were again doing walk-downs of safety systems throughout the plant just to be sure there were no other surprises. Soon the entire process for start-up of the power plant would begin all over again if the regulators allowed it. The weather predictions indicated that hot weather would be arriving soon, and the electricity that West Isles generated would be sorely needed. The company had a couple of gas turbine power generating units off-line for maintenance, so backup supply was limited. Therefore, the utility had to buy power off the grid at twice the cost. Other areas in the country were having an unprecedented demand also, and there was a fear that rolling blackouts would be necessary if West Isles wasn't up and running soon.

The FBI and the utility held a joint press conference where they provided information on the activities of Milo Parker and Norm Callaway. Only generalizations were provided, and there was no mention of the connection to the People for a Safe World. Margaret Colliers knew that this information would only whet the interest of the press, but she felt strongly that whatever could be shared should be shared as soon as possible. The FBI had agreed to move quickly on the investigation so that the full story could be discussed soon and preferably before the election.

Harry Clemons and others in the security department were going over the actions taken yesterday in response to Milo's actions. An elite team of inspectors from the NRC's office in Washington DC had arrived to go over the situation so they could provide a special report for the president of the United States. It was not clear if President Reagan would decide on the fate of West Isles' start-up, but everyone hoped that he would not interfere and leave the decision to the technical experts. All other nuclear power plants across the country had been put on alert but were allowed to continue operating as long as certain conditions did not exist at their facilities. The conditions specified were not discussed since they fell under the "safeguard security" requirements of confidentiality.

Earlier in the day, Jerry had seen the company's psychiatrist arrive for a meeting with Harry Clemons in the security building. He figured the arrival had to do with Milo Parker and how he got through the security screening program and personality profile examination to work at West Isles. It was clear to many that Milo was off kilter in more ways than one when they worked with him, and one of the changes would be to require the reporting of unusual behavior of employees to management. Most did not want to rat out their coworkers, and managers were fearful of lawsuits if individuals' behavior was misjudged. The security clearance process was already cumbersome and costly and probably would become even more so because of what Milo did. Federal regulations would be required to protect managers, and specific instructions would be needed to ensure success. Sawyer mentioned to Lindy that he had been invited to participate in the preparation of these new regulations and hoped that he would have to return to West Isles for work-related reasons.

Unfortunately for Lindy, the NRC also sent out their health physics experts from the DC office to do an unannounced inspection of the radiation safety program at West Isles. This required her to be at work rather than having a nice quiet day lying at the side of the pool as she had planned. A female NRC inspector was sitting at one of the desks in the dosimetry office, going through every piece of paper in file folders that were lying in a stack on the desk. Occasionally, Lindy saw her taking notes, and she had asked questions about some of the reports. The inspector had identified a few small errors, but so far appeared to be satisfied with what she saw. She would most likely head over to the security office to crosscheck the dosimetry records against the security records after this.

The inspector was also very interested in the records from the outage that Lindy had used to determine that Milo Parker and the murdered man may have been in the waste gas decay tank room at the same time. Copies of these reports were made for her. Lindy provided a summary of the estimated radiation dose that individuals involved in yesterday's activities had received. Don Ryder, the radiological engineer, worked up an estimate on the potential doses for Lindy, Sawyer, Marcus Laiden, Milo Parker, and several of the security guards. Lindy and Sawyer were estimated to have received 1.5 rem, based on the time they spent in the wraparound room and the dose measurements taken in the area. Radiation levels were not significantly elevated near the remote control panel, so Marcus Laiden had limited exposure, about 100 mrem. One security guard had over 1 rem recorded on his pencil dosimeter since he had been assigned to the minus-80 level for several hours. Other security guards had only a couple hundred millirem. Thankfully, none of them had exceeded the 3-rem maximum limit for the current quarter. No special reports were needed, except for Milo Parker. Ryder estimated Milo Parker's exposure to be around 700 rem, mostly due to his close contact with the diffuser panel, which had only recently been removed from the reactor vessel and was thus highly radioactive. The dose that is estimated to cause death in 50 percent of those exposed is 300 rem for the whole body for the average man. At 700 rem, Milo didn't stand a chance. Interesting enough, if this dose of 700 rem were spread out over several years, with many small doses given periodically, it would not be lethal. With smaller dose increments, the body has time to repair itself before the next exposure. A large amount of radiation over a short period of time devastates so many cells in the body that recovery is not possible.

After reviewing records for several hours, the female inspector left the trailer. Lindy was scheduled to attend an exit interview with the NRC inspectors late in the afternoon and knew that the lead inspector would need to compile a summary prior to that meeting using the information obtained by the female inspector.

The NRC exit meeting began sharply at 5:00 PM. The lead inspector was the director of the regional NRC office, Marvin North, and was well-known by the power plant workers to be a by-the-book inspector. Sometimes what was required by regulations wasn't sensible, but it wouldn't matter to Marvin North. Today the director got right to the discussion of violations other than those related to the security program. Those violations would be discussed behind closed doors with the department managers.

"The first violation is obvious. It is the catastrophic overexposure of Mr. Milo Parker, now deceased. This is a Level V violation. However, considering the circumstances, the normal penalty fine will be cut in half," said North, speaking rather casually, as if he were doing nothing more important than ordering off a menu.

Cahill, the plant manager, shifted in his chair, his face turning slightly red. The normal fee for a Level V violation was $1,000,000. There was no higher violation level. Cahill looked as if he were ready to argue, but instead he held back, knowing it would be of no use now. Later he would negotiate with the Washington, DC staff for a fairer evaluation of this violation. A Level V violation should only apply to a situation where gross negligence was involved in the overexposure and not to the voluntary and willful situation that Milo had knowingly put himself in.

North continued. "The second violation is for the lack of following dosimetry procedures when entering controlled radiation areas. Ms. Andrews and Mr. McMillan entered the minus-80 wraparound room without a self-reading dosimeter. In addition, a radiation work permit was not prepared before the entry, and significant radiation exposure was incurred. This is a Level II violation times two; however, again, the circumstances can allow the fine to be reduced."

Lindy cringed in her seat as others carefully glanced at her to see her reaction. To be named as the person that caused a violation was the lowest thing a worker could have happen to them, to say the least. Lindy screamed to herself, "But it was an emergency!"

Maddog could not hold back after hearing this recitation of the violation. "Are you kidding me, Mr. North? Do you realize what was prevented because of the fast thinking on the part of those two?"

"Yes, I do, but ..."

"And that we would be dealing with the much bigger problem of why we asked the nearby residents to evacuate when there would have been no reason to? Do you realize the stress and potential harm the public was saved? Ms. Andrews' fast actions prevented that from happening. If she had waited to prepare an RWP and grab a dosimeter, they would have been too late. Does that not figure into your thinking?"

"Procedures were not followed. That's a violation, I'm sorry," replied Mr. North, appearing not at all fazed by the comments. Lindy could see in Maddog's eyes that he would also be fighting this one, and she hoped he succeeded in getting the violation removed from the list. The violation report would need to be drafted and approved before the violations became final, giving Maddog time to talk with the director's superior.

North continued with a few more Level I violations and then ended the meeting. It appeared to Lindy that, all things considered, the violations would not prevent the plant from going back online. The final verdict would be whether the security program had any substantial violations that would require a fix before start-up. She would hear soon enough the outcome and hoped for the best.

Lindy walked back to the auxiliary building with Al Jensen.

"Lindy, what am I going to do with you? I can't seem to keep you out of trouble."

"Yeah, boss, what are you going to do with me?"

"I don't know," he said laughing lightly. "Unfortunately, you may still have more opportunities for disrupting the calm atmosphere around here."

"What do you mean? And what calm atmosphere?"

"That reporter wants to interview the people who assisted in stopping Milo. I think he may have heard you had some involvement. He asked to interview you and a few others."

"No, not again! His misquotes from the last article still haunt me! Industry friends from around the country are still calling, asking why I made such stupid statements. Please don't make me go through it again."

"We can talk more later after the FBI gets more information out. Why don't you go home now and take a day off and think about it. Remember that what you did was good for West Isles, and it would be good to tell your story and our side of it."

"Trying to guilt me into it?"

"Me? No way. But McMillan has already agreed to the interview— that may be good enough." Lindy's heart missed a beat when she heard Sawyer's name, and she made a small smile that she hoped Al did not notice.

"Okay, I'll think about it," said Lindy as she turned around to head back through the security building to get her things and head home. She was glad to hear that Sawyer would be around for a while longer.

*　　*　　*　　*

Tom Mietner sat uncomfortably in the chair across from Greg Montague. Montague was tapping a pencil against the edge of his desk, smoking a cigarette and gazing at Tom through the smoke swirls rising from the cigarette. This was the first time Montague had agreed to meet at campaign headquarters.

"I gather from the FBI's press conference that your guy did not come through for you. Is that right?" Montague said.

"I have not heard from him, so I'm assuming his plan did not work.

There should have been a major accident that threatened the safety of nearby residents, but something must have gone wrong."

"Now that's an understatement. There were some undercurrents at the FBI press conference that seemed to indicate some questionable actions on the part of a mysterious man who held a family hostage. This is not good, not good at all." Montague said calmly, although his eyes had taken on an unforgiving squint.

"Yes, it sounds very troublesome, but I hear the description of the person is very vague—could be anyone," said Mietner, his hands now shaking.

Montague smashed his cigarette butt deliberately into his ashtray. "I think you know what you need to do. Where did you come from? Some town in Oklahoma?"

"Yes, Stillwater, Oklahoma."

Montague walked around the desk, and as Mietner stood up, he whispered in his ear, "I never want to see your face again. And if you even mention me or Rackerby, we will find you. Am I clear?"

"Yes, sir." Mietner quickly left through the back entrance of the building. Mietner considered his options as he drove away: take the first flight back to Stillwater and go into hiding, or go to the police and start talking. He decided that Stillwater wasn't such a bad place after all and headed to his house to pack.

Chapter 35

A CROWD HAD GATHERED ON the back patio at Roadhouse to watch the returns on election night. It was almost eight o'clock, and the early election results would be reported soon. The heat of the day was just a memory. A faint yellow-orange was lingering to the west but quickly losing ground to deep reds and purples. A waitress was lighting a candle on a table. The television on a cart near the bar entry was not yet turned on.

Every available worker from West Isles was there. Only those on shift or sleeping in anticipation of the night shift to come were missing. Lydia and Marcus were sitting together at a small table in the corner, sipping their drinks, holding hands, and watching everyone. Marcus was not smoking and instead was aggressively chewing gum, which Lindy assumed had to be some type of antismoking aid. There was a group of mechanics at a back table at the opposite end of the room, drinking, talking loudly, and occasionally attempting to throw each other over the balcony into the slough below. Thumper was at a table with his wife, Betty, who was talking animatedly to Jane seated to her left. Betty spent all day at home with the kids and looked forward to this opportunity for adult conversation. She didn't notice that Thumper's foot started tapping whenever one of the young women who worked in the office at West Isles walked by or that his eyes followed them across the room. Lindy doubted Betty would have been surprised at the behavior even if she had noticed. Betty knew he was a big talker but was sure he didn't have it in him to act; he surely never got the opportunity.

As crazy as these people were, Lindy would still miss them if it turned out the plant was shut down and she had to move on. She might even miss Fred Ingalls, but then she thought otherwise. Lindy had talked to him earlier and had to keep from busting a gut over the baloney he was feeding her. Ingalls was telling her and everyone else that it was information from him that had led to exposing Norm Callaway as the real killer. It was true that he had told the FBI about the money scam, but the second part about him helping the FBI put two and two together was hogwash. However, it wasn't generally known what Milo had said before dying, and the follow-up in the instrument calibration lab that led to finding the murder weapon had not been released yet because the investigation was still under way. Lindy quickly made an excuse and sat in the lone seat next to Dottie, leaving Ingalls to walk away.

Al Jensen was now at the television, cruising the channels and adjusting the volume. "Okay, everyone, they may have some early returns soon," he said. Most ignored Al and continued their conversations.

Jack Huston, the radiation protection technician who seemed most worried about losing his job, sat in a nearby chair and stared apprehensively at the television. Al found a news channel. Jack saw that the propositions were being reported, and he immediately jumped up and yelled, "Hey, everybody! It's on! Listen up!"

At this everyone quieted down, took a seat, and cautiously watched the television. The announcer was discussing Proposition P and appeared to be going in alphabetical order. The proposition on whether to shut down West Isles or keep it operating was an advisory vote, since the decision to operate was ultimately up to the utility board, but all the members had said that they would honor the wishes of the people. The proponents of Proposition R had argued that it would be cheaper to shut West Isles down and replace it with natural gas power plants. Natural gas costs were at an all-time low and were competitive with the costs of nuclear. Besides, they argued, nuclear power plants were just too dangerous, and to be safe, they all needed to be shut down.

A yes vote meant that the plant should be shut down. A no vote would indicate a vote of confidence for the plant and keep it running. A yes vote also meant that most everyone here on the patio would lose their jobs, some more quickly than others, and some possibly within a week's time. A lot was at stake for those congregated on that deck, and deep anxiety was visible on most faces. Some West Isles workers had already moved on to new jobs in previous months, not being able to live with the uncertainty of the situation. Lindy had never experienced a circumstance where her future rested in the hands of the voting public. She was lucky in that she was single, for it would be relatively easy for her to find another job somewhere in the country. Even though she felt unwelcome in the outside community, she didn't want to leave. Nevertheless, she had found herself analyzing strangers at the grocery store, trying to figure out whether they wanted to fire her or were intelligent human beings who looked to the future and embraced the importance of nuclear power. She hoped her dislike of more earthy looking individuals who looked liked environmentalists did not show. She took another swig of her beer and reached for Dottie's hand, who was sitting next to her. Dottie was shaking. Lindy got close and held her tightly, mostly so that Dottie wouldn't notice how much she was shaking too. She observed a spider about ready to crawl on Dottie's arm and quickly swatted it away. It reminded her that she hadn't had a dream about spiders for several weeks.

Someone turned up the volume on the television. "... and Proposition Q, which would authorize an additional $600 million in bonds for school building improvements, has 42 percent yes votes, and 49 percent no votes, with 5 percent of precincts reporting. This one is too close to call as of now. And next, Proposition R, which has been a very controversial measure that will provide an advisory vote on whether to shut down the West Isles Nuclear Power Plant. Do we have those results?" said the woman announcer.

Proposition R was written on the screen, but the percentages of yes and no votes were blank. The announcer listened for a minute to her earpiece and continued. "Okay folks, it will be just a minute for results. This proposition took a dramatic turn, as you will recall, with the attempted hijack of the West Isles facility just two weeks ago. There have been allegations that the Yes on Prop R committee, along with People for a Safe World, may have had some connection with the conspirator who was an employee at West Isles. The FBI is currently investigating People for a Safe World and ... oh, here we go folks: yes has 42 percent of the votes and no has 63 percent, with ..."

Everyone on the deck exploded with cheers! They were winning by a big margin! There was no way for the yes votes to catch up with that large a margin. There were hugs and kisses of joy all around, especially from Thumper, who had now conveniently found himself standing next to the document girls, his foot striking the floor with little taps throughout the hugging. The mechanics showed their joy by throwing a junior mechanic over the deck and into the slough, hooting and hollering. Dottie had tears in her eyes as she jumped up and down with Lindy. Lindy danced with her beer bottle held above her head. Others joined her.

In her exuberance Lindy failed to notice right away that Chris Sievers was celebrating with her. When she looked up, she saw Chris smiling at her. They had not talked since the eventful day when he was acting as the shift supervisor.

"Lindy, you are looking happy tonight!" Chris was clearly trying to make amends.

"Yes, we certainly have a reason to celebrate, don't you think?"

"I agree. But to have someone to share it with would be even better," said Chris, trying to sound casual.

Lindy stopped her dancing to take a long hard look at Sievers.

"Well, then, you'd better go find someone," Lindy said, holding her chin high. "I hear there's a new girl in accounting you might like." And with that, Lindy turned and started dancing with Jack. She felt triumphant. Never again would she be used and thrown aside. She wouldn't settle again for whomever she happened to land with.

A waitress fought through the dancing mob and yelled in Lindy's ear that she had a phone call. Lindy worked her way back through the crowd into the bar area and over to the telephone receiver sitting on the bar.

"Lindy, Sawyer. Just had to call when I heard the news." He had returned to DC several days earlier with a promise to keep in touch. They had spent many nights together, and it had been brutal to say good-bye. Lindy wondered why she continued to put herself through the pain, but she thought this was one person she would work hard to be with.

"Yes, we are all celebrating here. The no votes have got a good lead, and the local news agencies are projecting that the proposition will fail, which means the plant will stay in operation," Lindy said.

"Good! Congratulations! With all the problems, I was worried that it wasn't going to go well. But I guess people always like an underdog. Strange days, indeed."

"Yeah, once everyone realized that there was foul play, I think they decided to give us another chance. We may battle another referendum in the future, but I think we will do okay. Any more news on who Milo was working with?"

"I believe I know who was helping Milo, but we have no evidence to link him. Mrs. Laiden said that Tom Mietner looked like the man who held them hostage, but she couldn't be sure."

"And Tom Mietner is?"

"Someone who volunteered for People for a Safe World. Records show he provided a lot of financial support. He was also seen at events that supported Rackerby for Governor, but that would be expected since Rackerby supported the shutdown of West Isles. And the founder of People for a Safe World, Art Bigsbee, hasn't been helpful. So all we have on Mietner is that he donated money to a cause he believed in—not enough to take it to the bank," said Sawyer, disappointedly. He hated that the power players sponsoring Milo could not be brought to justice.

"Well, you may not put all the bad guys in jail, but at least your reports have gotten the power plants to enact new security policies. With the added background checks and improved psychological testing, we shouldn't have any Milos working in the nuclear industry in the future," said Lindy. And as an afterthought, she asked, "Will you be visiting us soon?"

"Unfortunately not. That's another reason that I called. I've got a new assignment that will keep me in the southeast for a while. I was hoping to return, but ... the bosses think this other matter is a higher priority. I'm sorry ..."

"Umm, I understand," said Lindy laconically.

"I have vacation time saved up. When this post is done, we could meet. How's that?" asked Sawyer.

"Sounds good! I know where there's a private beach with no one around but some seagulls."

"I am looking forward to having the time to watch those seagulls. I'll bring the sunscreen. You bring the beer."

"It's a date," Lindy said. She wished they were together right now. She wanted to kiss him and hold him. She didn't know if she could wait "awhile" for him to get back. But she had no choice.

"I need to go, okay? Take care, Mr. FBI Man," she said, her voice quivering.

"Will do," he said. "Be safe. Bye."

Lindy hung up the phone and paused, facing the wall where the telephone cradle hung. It will be okay, she told herself. At least there was something to look forward to.

Lindy turned and walked back out to the patio. The party was going strong, and she could not help but put a smile on her face. She joined Jack Huston and the other dancers. The television was on, but nobody was watching it. The screen showed that Rackerby was behind by a large margin.

- The End -

LaVergne, TN USA
05 May 2010
181656LV00006B/12/P